THE NAKED ANARCHIST

THE NAKED ANARCHIST
LLUIS FERNANDEZ

◀◀◀◀GMP▶▶▶▶

Original Catalan edition
    L'Anarquista Nu
    Edicions 62, Barcelona, 1979.

First British edition published 1990 by
    GMP Publishers Ltd,
    P O Box 247,
    London N17 9QR.

World Copyright © 1979 Lluís Fernàndez

Translation, World Copyright © 1990
Dominic Lutyens / Triangle Translations

Distributed in North America by
    Alyson Publications Inc.,
    40 Plymouth Street
    Boston, MA 02118, USA.

Distributed in Australia by
    Stilone Pty Ltd.,
    P O Box 155,
    Broadway, NSW 2007, Australia.

British Library Cataloguing in Publication Data

Fernàndez, Lluís *1945–*
    The Naked Anarchist.
    I. Title II. L'Anarquista nu.
    English
    849.9354 [F]

    ISBN 0-85449-139-2

Printed and bound in the EC on environmentally-friendly paper by Norhaven
    A/S, Viborg, Denmark.

Typeset by Fine Line Publishing Services, Witney, Oxfordshire.

"Oh, noblest and most civilised Valencia; in all Catalonia no city matches you for your wanton and lascivious ways."
    M. Bandello (16th century)

"Who can say that they are not unhappy,
Or have not at some time been saddened, embittered,
Bound as we are by the dictates of fate.
Sombre thoughts comparable
Only to the world's darkest regions
Reveal mental turbulence and irrational thoughts.
These are like those of an insane man who,
Enraged by the most oppressive pain,
Finds the cause to be his *love*."
    Ansias March, XXXIX

"No one listen to my voice and sad tone,
With its mingled sighs and tears,
For deep in my breast is a
Searing pain such as I have never felt."
    Villamediana, *White Ballad*

"Preaching in Seu, Master Castanyoli, a priest among sinners, said that a dreadful vice had come to his notice and that, for the sins of mankind, God would inflict on their lands, pestilence, war and famine... God was most offended because he knew that certain people indulged in the sin of sodomy, and speedily did he advise his ministers to punish the guilty."
    Memoirs, 22nd July, 1519

Epistles, billets-doux, letters and even telegrams. Maxims and intimate notes, missives, circulars, minutes and jottings – all kinds of correspondence appear in this book entitled 'The Naked Anarchist'. Unclean tales, slanderous gossip, unhappy tales of miscarried love affairs, follies, tragedies – all these are written down by their characters in an ephemeral form, since they know that to outlive them would be to commit a dishonour.

Amsterdam, 30th August, 1976

I can still hear the rain joyfully beating against my window. I'm counting off the seconds of every minute, it seems as if the clocks have stopped. The night looks like a ball of black rubber, strolling mockingly before my eyes. And now it's taken off only to disappear down the drain which empties into the canal. I can hear the tap in the bathroom dripping as it fills the bath.

I've bought five packs of suppositories so I should have enough. I've got to kill my pain – if I'm going to succeed in killing death. I think of the tenderness of our final embrace, before a mirror bejewelled with condensation and sweat. A misted mirror, reflecting only the clouded remnants of ambiguous fantasy. Nothing can disturb the silence which absence generates, the silence of water as it both animates and enshrouds mirrors and glass surfaces, tender as down on a chick's back soaked by the rain. Silence is broken only by the movement of the water in the canal and the reflections cast on it by the light from my ceiling.

Down on the canal I can see letters, sentences, the absurd language of a will whose style dooms it to banality. Bleeding into its background of soaking paper, it has become as futile as a message in a bottle. As the sheets of paper float away awash, its last few paragraphs seem to impress themselves on the water's forgetful, *trompe l'oeil* surface. To write a will there must be ritual, and to die there must be mirrors.

Dear Aurelio,

It's four days now since you left and I still wonder how I could have got by without my heart fatally skipping a beat. How my memory torments me with its cinematic twists – like a diorama of flashing and painfully repetitive images. One nihilistic flashback haunts me in particular: you in the foreground, in close-up, at one moment; in the background the next.

I can see the scene now quite clearly. How, when seen in the distance do the figures of people shrink so! Suddenly, I found myself on the wrong side of the mirror, helpless. The nearer I tried to come to you, the further I became. Prey to the duplicity of distances, I have become wary of false perspectives.

When you had gone for good and were standing there on the pavement, my hands ventured a pathetic, tiny gesture: without the aid of speech, they resorted to snatching the air and reclaiming in vain the distance that separated us.

I'm on my way home and that flashback, that storyboard's here again. It's outdoors. Daytime in Caudillo Square. Aurelio gets into a car. He starts it – the engine revs up. He turns off to the right and disappears. Long shot. Background.

It's noon by the town hall clock. It seems illogical, but the bustling city around me doesn't appear to register imminent disaster. Obviously, the world is indifferent to such insignificant, everyday tragedies.

Here, at home, life has come to a standstill.

There's the sound of voices from all corners, sounds detaching

9

themselves stealthily from the ceiling and curtains, words hovering above the bedside table. The shower is still on. In the unmade bed, an unfinished sentence, lingering like the vestiges of a party, reflects itself in the mirror, fixes itself, indelibly resistant to time.

I must remember: only time heals. I must hang all my hopes on time. At dusk, I passed the time walking along those streets that were so familiar to us. God it was hard! Every street left the aftertaste of memories, of your words, of irrevocable footsteps, now opaque and lost to time. In the face of these memories, I muster all my strength to resist suicidal thoughts.

What should I do? To regain happiness I would have to deny myself my memories, undergo a lobotomy? Should I hold on to them, and then be prepared to live a life of misery? Or should I rename the city's streets? Remodel the city's architecture? Or cut down the endless rows of monotonous poplars.

In my despair, I'm desperate to see a doctor!

On the table where I'm sitting every piece of paper, every pencil has stayed in its original place. In fact all the objects we knew are now autonomous – they refuse to be disturbed. There's the white rubber, the unopened tobacco pouch, yesterday's paper, the stapler, the scissors and the trimmings off the photo you took with you, the full ashtray, the black rotring pen and the now silenced, secret message you wrote to me on a bookcover; one chair left where it was, close to another one and even the tiles on the floor recall your footsteps, still fresh and dear to me.

You've turned my home into a hostile place. You've destroyed what harmony I once knew. Everything finds comfort here except for me. I've decided, therefore, to take charges out against you for neglect of domicile, for disturbance of my ecosystem, for persistent harassment and for suggestion of alcoholism.

So beware the consequences!

Now I see how backgrounds conspire to make people walking away shrink beyond recognition.

Aurelio, my precious!

I am a transformed WOMAN at last! If you saw me you wouldn't recognise that stupid and weedy boy you once knew. I'm ready to hit Mayor Street. Tremble, all you passers-by – here comes your new sidewalk queen, a pavement-pounder, fearsome, fat and unspeakable. "Thunder thighs Pipi!" they shout. And that's not all! You've no idea what a success I've been: I haven't been able to keep the crowds away since the day I set foot in this street of passion! We were made for revenge, a revenge against those stupid, countless moralists who have wanted to keep us under wraps for so long.

What's more, it's helped me to overcome that complex I had about my body. I hated everything about it: tubby, deformed, beneath contempt; my tits revoltingly pneumatic, my belly a stack of spare tyres. Worst of all my arse! My God what a sight I must have been! Of course, I felt humiliated. I locked myself at home. I was practically broken from so much crying, not to say by my fits of rage. So many mirrors were shattered because they dared reflect my hideous, bulbous body!

But it's all over now. "Up yours!" I said to the world one day. With that I left home and a mortified mother and took to the street with only a bundle of possessions to my name.

I picked up some money I'd saved from work and stashed away in the office and legged it to Lulú's. "Lulú, darling," I asked her. "I'd like a complete change of image. What would you suggest?"

There and then Lulú pulled out an entire collection from her dressing-up chest and gave me a complete makeover – not easy, I admit.

"Have faith," she said. "Nothing's impossible. Just look at what I did with Cenicientona in five minutes flat. Remember what a mess *she* was!" Lulú scrutinised me, looked me up and down, first tying a bottle green sash round my waist to cover up my disloyal spare tyre. Next, she put a black velvet choker with a cameo round my neck.

It had originally been worn by Lulú's grandmother, Rosario (the one with which she'd pulled so many men just as I wanted to do myself!) And there was a corset. Since it was bordered with a pattern of whales, Lulú assured me it would make me look more svelte! "You know what I mean. Pipi, as I see it you ought to be going for the Modigliani look. It's either that or you'll be lumbered with looking like Long Tall Sally – which as far as I'm concerned you might as well forget!"

With my nails now painted and a hat to conceal my rat's tail hair, I was ready to leave the fitting room intent on stealing the part of Scarlett O'Hara from Vivien Leigh. But no, Lulú was kidding herself. I'll never be Scarlett O'Hara, nor a scarlet woman for that matter. Much less will I ever get gorgeous Gable kissing me, pressing his masculine, clipped moustache against me. With any luck, I told myself, I'll at least look like Manrujita Díaz in the film *Pelusa*. Not ideal, I know, but it would be an improvement on my past self. As it was only the first day I'd changed my image, I took heart and when I got home I had a shower, stripped myself of my ludicrous get-up and told myself like a good friend: "Don't be so silly, you're the hottest thing on two legs. Unadulterated sex. Dynamite. Get out and flaunt it and stop cowering in the closet."

Wearing the subtlest stroke of lipstick, a streak of blue eyeliner, an exotic coat of mauve nail varnish, a Mama Cass tunic and a bag bearing an activist slogan, I became, quite without knowing it, Pipi Yaguer herself, reservoir of the erotic in motion.

When I'm feeling *really* blasé, Aurelio, I'll send you a photo! Nothing to it, I thought, but get out onto d'Enmig Street – you don't need me to tell you what Castellón is like at half past six – in hot pursuit of sex. In that street of surreptitious glances, covert desires and secret yearnings, sex is the best way to keep depression at bay. I was lucky first time: a hunk, butch beyond belief, asked me back. As his guest star for that night's *Late Late Show* I was as if quite smitten.

That was just the start: I get so many calls these days, I can now confidently consider myself a fully fledged call girl.

Bonnie Moronie's in luck: flesh is back in fashion and people really want something to get their teeth into, which suits me – I've got enough of it to sink a battleship!

I'm writing to you in bed. Mr Incommensurable Hunk, lying beside me, sends you his regards.

I spend more time thinking of you than you really deserve, you bastard!

Love from your friend,
Pipi (Enrique)

LETTER 3
To Aurelio Santonja from Lulú Bon
Valencia, 28th August, 1975

Dear Aurelio,

When a Hollywood star takes a pot shot at a lover in a posh
restaurant, the repercussions are without doubt as predictable as
the sensationalist coverlines which this week *El Caso* devoted to
the story of Korea.

The story goes that Korea gave herself up to the police after
having shot her lover, Andres Vergara, with a shotgun. It had
come to her notice that he had been having it away with a bit of
fluff, a member of Valencia's jet-setting élite. If that wasn't
enough he'd also had the gall to flaunt his find not only in
Valencia's most exclusive restaurants but also, quite openly at
the Opera, and at both the Polo and Tennis Clubs!

The scandal, filtering as it did from club to club, took time to
ferment. But when it erupted, there was only one way it would
all end – in violence. What really did it was the way that he
paraded his new boyfriend. This he did with such recklessness
that his actions were nothing if not defiant.

Not since the year of the Ruiz de Liori murders, the murderer
who carved up his victims and put them into plastic milk churns,
has there been a scandal on this scale. Normally cossetted, the
upper classes and well-to-do households here have been once
again forced to acknowledge that life is not as cosy as they would
like to think.

Although I don't hold out much hope, I would like to think
that society will look kindly on what was in fact a *crime passionnel*.
Hopefully she won't die lovelorn but will continue to act self-

destructively in love's name. Long live love!

I'm home again after having tried to find out more about the Korea case. No luck, I'm afraid, but I'll keep you up to date. Now I'm off to slag it as God wills! I'm wearing all my glad rags and hope, as I sit with my glass of anis, that old slob Roger will call me. I'm staring absent-mindedly at the cardigan hanging on my clothes stand which sits, with its intertwining spirals, on the plaster console fronted with its Baroque arabesques in *or maché*. As I clutch my little purse, a hesitant, jaded smile lingers at the corners of my mouth. My purse is perfect for evenings out. With its discreet arrangement of sequins scattered casually against a black satin ground, it's wonderfully restrained. In my preference for sober simplicity, I've decided I'm like a Russian princess.

I take out my cigarette and the lighter you gave me, my precious Dupont. I light up and as I do so my eyes light up at the same time. How exquisitely they're made up, down to the last detail, outlined as they are with a pencil and Rimmel and finally given extra definition with green eyeliner. I never skimp on time or effort. My eyes are two glowing pupils. I let my lighter go out and its flames die away. I breathe deeply. I purse my lips and take a drag on my mauve cigarette with its gold cigarette holder – and inhale deeply. As the smoke blows out, I warm up the little corner of the room you knew so well. The room is as you left it: it still has its distinctive smell of honey-sweet Chanel perfume.

Aurelio, I can hear the doorbell! That must be him.

Ciao, baby.

Lulú strikes again!

Write soon,
Lulú Bon

LETTER 4
To Aurelio Santonja from Lulú Bon
Valencia, 4th September, 1975

Aurelio darling,

You asked after Pepe. I take it you mean 'bedhopper' Pepe. What a strange girl she is! Events have taken quite a turn and she's vanished off the face of the earth. You wanted to know if there was any news of her... Well, here goes. Quite simply, the smell of ecclesiastical candles sends her wild. I love hearing what stories she has to tell me, trivial as they might be, as she sits there behind her glasses as thick as bottles and with her pious Jesuitic air. Her hands are always entwined and her posture calm and relaxed. And what with her constant commuting between confessional and communion, her mouth has become quite misshapen with so much spiritual grimacing.

   Having observed how often she's been to the church of Buen Remedio recently, the one between Chinatown and Peu de la Creu Street and when I saw the priest, a man, incidentally of breathtaking corpulence, I instantly sussed the situation!

   You can imagine then why Pepe so wanted help with the evening mass, to oblige with his spriritual duties, with the memorial services, with the viatica and even with the early morning rosary. Pepe's strategy is indeed a protracted and above all a deliberately 'self-sacrificing' one. But Pepe says she always achieves her aim. Her ruse was to play the doubting Catholic – with its appeal, of course, to spiritual support – and then with slow deliberation to strike up a friendship. Her web spun she has slowly but surely succeeded in trapping her prey. Thus has Pepe achieved her goal. You should have seen the church's chaplain for yourself! He may be a slight man but he's wiry all the same. At forty he still looks very young for his age. As Pepe has found to her delight, his sunny and sporty expression goes hand in hand with his readiness and willingness to lend a hand.

After only fifteen days of involvement in the liturgy, Pepe went to work on 'confessing'. Cramming her confessions with sob stories and indulgent little foibles, she found a place in his heart. She stopped short of nothing, confessing guilt of miscarried loves and of seedy, furtive desires. Only God will ever know what fiendish stories so quickly precipitated their love affair – making love in the sacristy – exemplary Christian behaviour, you might say! – amongst the cassocks, chalices, patens, dalmatics, waterproof surplices, stoles, salvers, the sacred Host itself sent floorwards in their abandon, ditto the silver Holy Grail with its specious gems and plastic precious stones.

But wait for it – this isn't the half of it. Not even the Marchioness of Montreuil herself could have dreamt up so well-planned, so ingenious, so successful a plan as Pepe concocted. It all started the day I was in North Station. I'd picked up a boy with whom I was extremely taken. I was so fascinated by his charm, so taken by his kindness and wit that I took him back to Pepe's. There where there were a few friends, but I could be sure that I'd be welcome. When I introduced him to Pepe he was struck by one thing – his 'smell'. His olfactory 'vibes', he told me in an aside, signalled to him that he came from a rarefied community. His tone betraying growing excitement, he speculated that the boy was from military barracks or a religious seminary. You wouldn't believe how much Pepe gets turned on by lace, by the hems of chasubles, by satin, by the damasks of ecclesiastical vestments, the smell of black cassocks, incense, burning candles, confessionals and the antique scent of wooden crucifixes!

Personally, I smelt nothing strange. There was no reason for me to think my sense of smell was not as sensitive as his. So I proceeded without ado. We sat down on a functional, some would say uncomfortable sofa, upholstered in a sprigged cretonne, and had a drink.

The other people in the room, meanwhile, complied with my plans. They receded discreetly into the room's corners and the

17

lights were dimmed to a subtle glow. I looked at the boy's eyes and also saw what a tender mouth he had. His lips parted succulently as he spoke. I was becoming more and more attracted to his body: he was so youthful that he seemed to bear the mark of immortality.

He looked into my eyes and his eyelashes quivered. I returned his look with a burning intensity. Then he would venture a smile which hovered timidly at the extremities of his lips.

Was I in luck at last? Who could tell? Optimistically I told myself I was as I let my arm slide up behind his shoulder and come to rest gently on his back. Both my knees moved, no longer deadweight, and brushed against his, sending electric shivers up my spine. Then they went back to where they'd been. My arm could feel his shoulder quivering which made me think the feeling was mutual. "He only has to tremble with anticipation," I told myself, "and he must be gay."

As we talked I changed the tone of conversation, making it more intimate, more personal. Edging up to him, I whispered sibilant sounds in his ears, words incoherent and fragmented. I watched as he responded positively, warming to this charmed circle which I had created and which my soft murmurings had generated in this intangible game of mutual seduction. Bit by bit, sexual messages were being infused into his every pore, into the orifice of his ear which my mouth was by now virtually caressing. As my left hand pressed against his muscular frame and allowed itself to wander over the boy's groin, so did his pulse gather speed and his body heave the more quickly.

My nerves were on edge; my flesh was beginning to melt as fast as ice cream in a hot oven. My pulse rate was thudding audibly. My breathing was intermittent, my breath hot as a steam-filled sauna. My cock was by now restrained only by the waistband of my underpants. I decided to go full throttle and take the plunge with a frontal attack on his crotch. At that moment there was a terrible silence. His body held back! The suspense..! What if I hadn't played my cards right? Another record started to play, the needle crackling discordantly along its initial grooves. Fortunately, a musical chord filled the vacuum of the room's silence; not only did his heart start to pound again but I could feel a growing bulge under my hand.

18

Suddenly, my heart lifted. I was filled with relief and joy. My lips went to meet his, as I began to undo his flies. But his mouth remained firmly, stubbornly closed. Like a locksmith, my lips glided over his mouth as if to prise onto his chin, climbing up to his ear where I began to bite at it gently while stroking his unyielding cock through his underpants. I knew, then, that until I had access to his mouth there was no way I would get at his meat.

Would I, I asked myself, have to ravage his mouth before his cock broke loose from its confines?

My wandering lips again reached for his face while he, stubbornly, kept his closed. I went from cheeks to ear and down again repeatedly until he began to give way and relax: very slowly my lips fused with his and now that they obediently parted, my tongue plunged deep into his throat, tasting, as it went, a certain dryness, as if, apprehensive, restraint was getting the better of him.

How young and virginal he seemed! And how uneasy he was! His tender lips tasted of the freshest milk, his skin as soft as a newly weaned baby. In the room's dim light, I could see, as if a ruddy sun dawning, his cock straining upwards, moist and glowing. I was taken aback by its sudden vigour and fantasised about how much I wanted him to fuck me! As far as I can remember, at that point, I ran my tongue from his chest down to the ridge of hair that links throat and navel until recklessly I reached his thicket of pubic hair. Suddenly, I devoured his cock. Struggling with its size, my mouth was forced to open wider and wider as I swallowed. (Whatever happened, I can be quite sure that my tongue was no longer down his throat!) On I sucked, my mouth pumping rhythmically, cyclically, without drawing breath, while his cock impaled my mouth. Both our hearts joined in a single act. Uninhibited, we were like open vowels. His apprenticeship in the grammar of sex was complete!

He mauled my back with love bites and bruises, although they felt to me like the softest caresses. I begged him to treat me rougher. As he did so my arse felt like a furnace from so much beating. Winding his legs round me, he began to ram my arse, making it smart. His cock probed the pit of my arse with such violence that I thought he would savage my prostate! (But at that

19

moment, I couldn't have cared less...) I was lying supine, strad-dled, feeling the most intense pleasure confounded by a tingling sensation that I can only describe as explosive, psychedelic. Lights flickered in my head intermittently, flashing, disappearing, a chromatic whirl which only crystallised when the thick current of his cream spurted out and flooded my body.

Next thing I knew, I felt sodden with sticky sweat – more to the point I was drenched in his irrepressible, incontainable spunk. When I fully 'came to', I ran my fingers through my hair, alarmed by my own disarray. (What loss of composure! Horrified I thought how Lana Turner would be turning in her grave now, appalled to see such disrespect for celluloid perfection!)

I remember that I cried. Whether these were tears of joy or of panic at my disarray, I'm not really sure. But I did definitely cry – even if my wits were sufficiently about me to utter, while sobbing, the mischievous knowing words, "You make love just like a priest".

Startled, he replied, "How do you know I am?"

Fortunately I managed to quell his curiosity, and soon we were fast asleep...

It was quite some time before I next saw him. But I soon heard that Pepe had been spreading rumours about what was only a trifle and when I bumped into him I confronted him about it.

You should have heard the passers-by cheering us on. It was like being at the Alcázar Theatre, complete with its wolf-whistling and vaudeville style audience. Pepe and I almost tore each other's hair out by the roots. I won absolutely.

Ferocious as we were when we started fighting, we finally made up. Why lose useful enemies, is what I say? To seal our friendship, and to bring the story to its conclusion, Aurelio, I gave him my priest's phone number and he took off jubilant as a successful exorcist.

That's all folks!

Love, hugs, lovebites, not to say a touch of spite from your old friend,
Lulú Bon

LETTER 5
To Aurelio Santonja from a stranger
Valencia, 19th September, 1975

Sunday, 13th
Feeling restless, I get up, my whole body soaked in sweat. I love you! It's 5.20 in the morning and it's still dark. Thinking of you keeps me awake. I think of you all the time as I sit here smoking. I can't think of anything but you.

Monday, 14th
I went to North Station to watch the trains go by. The green train you left in looked at me slyly from across the platform. They were washing it, wiping away your traces. Again, I could see your face slipping away in the crowd. I went back again in search of you.

Tuesday, 15th
I've bitten my nails to the quick. My nerves are playing havoc. I can't sit still: I walk around the house, along the passage like a caged bird. I'm lost without you, frustrated, dumb. I've had people ringing at the door three times but I can't answer it. I don't want to open it; I refuse. The phone's off the hook. It's six o'clock in the afternoon and I haven't eaten since Sunday. I just want to die. I feel like your prisoner and keeper at the same time.

Wednesday, 16th
Today I took the bed apart, smashed up the mattress and all the records we once liked listening to together. The bedroom looks as if a bomb's hit it. I can't swallow my food. Today I could only bring myself to drink orange juice. I tried to eat an apple but I

can't. I've been holding it in my hands and it's virtually rotten now. I'll just lie here on the floor. What difference will it make, anyway, I can't sleep.

Thursday, 17th
I'm going mad! I can feel my body giving way, my legs sagging. I'm starting to think that you'll never be back. Is that possible? I prefer to shut out the truth in the hope that it will anaesthetise the pain. I'm going to die of neglect, of starvation. I only had a few mirrors left but I've smashed them all now – they were reflecting your ghost. Yes, whenever I look at myself, I feel alienated, thinking of you and how far away you are. Have you forgotten about me already? Lie to me, tell me that you still love me!

Friday, 18th
I tried to slash my wrists. But I couldn't do it! I just couldn't! There's nothing left for me to destroy, nothing. No one rings at the door anymore. I think I'll soon be dead. How I hate you! Now I'm going to destroy my typewriter, pick it to pieces key by key...

LETTER 6
To Aurelio Santonja from Carlos Besada
Valencia, September 15th, 1975

Dear Aurelio,

I think the guy I met the other day at a Mozart recital at Santa
Catalina's Church would have been right up your street. He's
just the kind of Valencian country boy we've both had our eye
out for when we've been round the local villages. His skin is as
soft as duck's down and he looks at you with untainted tenderness.
He's sixteen, yet infinitely wise.

It was night-time and the church was packed with people in
dinner jackets and evening dress, a motley crowd ranging from
chi-chi bourgeois to trumped-up provincial. The first strains of
'Introibo al altare Dei' had begun. As I took in the crowd, my eyes
suddenly focussed on the figure of a boy who was walking in my
direction. Our eyes met and sparkled in that moment of 'recognition'. Gradually, I edged up to him until our bodies were
almost in contact. Standing as we were in the crowd, his arse
backed up against me, slowly. I was nervous, my knees were
shaking. I tried to hold my breath: if I'd breathed normally his
neck would have felt the blast of my breath! But then, without my
noticing, he came so close that my lips were brushing his musky
hair. As if by magic, the crowd was no more. We hardly noticed
the string orchestra, lost as we were in our frenzy! We were a
bubble of love in the midst of so many oblivious faces, unaware
of the opportunity which, ironically, the church had provided.
On the one hand, there was the rapt crowd, absorbed in the
concert, on the other there was the silent, private music of our
own making. In effect, we were restoring to the empty ritual of

23

the church its proper orgiastic substance.

I'm sure we were probably scared rigid of being discovered. But maybe that's what galvanised us, encouraged our abandon, made us act like children who misbehave and think nothing of the consequences since they're simply responding as they do to the most spontaneous and universal of desires. Suddenly the music became deafening. The church choir reached impossible crescendos which flowed over us, enhancing our passion, causing our bodies to fuse all the more. We were bound to one another: his arse now yearning to take my prick whole, changing from pith to pulp. It was like fruit which, at a bite, liquifies. Our skin, too, stood on end, as we shivered hot and cold. Plunging my hand down his flies – we'd both come at the same time – I felt his warm, moist spunk, and mine, too, viscous as his run down the inside leg of my flannel trousers.

I couldn't begin to describe my elation. Our two breathless hearts were beating in unison, our two bodies were clinging together like limpets. My lips went to his ear and I gripped him by the shoulders. He, meanwhile, leant back against my shoulder amorously, without turning, his farewell consistent with the anonymity of our encounter. The recital was at an end. Within a few seconds I'd lost him to the crowd without the opportunity to find out so common a detail as his name or the possibility of meeting him again! There it is, Aurelio. To think we never spoke a word to each other. It may sound stupid, Aurelio, but it's had a bad effect on me. I'd never thought just how much a threat this boy posed to my security. Here in my office, I sit stupefied, staring into space. Yes, the memory of that night haunts me. Anonymous as it was, I haven't felt such a strong rapport for ages.

Best wishes from your friend,
Carlos Besada

Why do you still write to me? Can you even remember?

LETTER 7
To Aurelio Santonja from the Adventuress of Macao
Valencia, September 17th, 1975

Dear Aurelio,

I recently heard that you have to be *forced* to leave home, you hate
the outside world so much. Your bosom pal, Lulú, has kept me
in the picture.

You've no idea how sorry I am to hear this, but life is a bitch
and no sooner do you wear your heart on your sleeve but
someone takes advantage. Matilde Belda, our official 'mistress of
scandals', is basing her book on the subject. She says it will form
part of a trilogy on domestic queens. What a storm that will
cause!

The book in question is to be called *How To Marry A Proletarian*.
A few nights ago I was round at his place looking through
the manuscript and saw that we'd all been mentioned to some
extent or other. It's a kind of in-depth analysis of the 'Valen-
ciana' – as well as a study of what special features we Valencian
as have as distinct from those of 'counterqueens' around the
globe. But don't think for a moment that Matilde's study is a
sociological one. Her research is more a form of metropolitan
anthropology than anything else: as she sees it, a subordinate,
albeit dignified gay subculture, suffers at the hands of its
oppressors.

I like her literary style: loving the Gothic as she does, it's a
cocktail of Joyce and Corín Tellado with a dash of Anita Loos.
No, I haven't forgotten the influence on Matilde's writing of our
own provincial, Valencian Baroque. Like Vicente Blasco Ibáñez,
Matilde writes both in Castilian and in the 'urban' Valencian

mode. She's got a tongue like a viper. And, as you know, she is very right-wing and very proud of it, too.

Don't worry about *your* particular involvement. She's changed all the names and even the places where everything happened. You'll be happy to hear that all references to real people have been adequately blurred.

I've never known anyone who people would so gladly see disposed of! She's a shit-stirrer, she's dangerous. Politically, she's even more reactionary than Doña Carmen Polo which I hardly think an appropriate ideology for a queen. I can't think of anything more contradictory. Although I know there are those who mistakenly think it is.

So engrossed is she in her studies that Matilde spends all day at home reading, writing and thinking. But to be a writer you've got to get out and about, experience life at first hand, do your research. You can't just swan through life like a dilettante, scraping by with a few superficial 'insights' here and a few 'ideas' there – even though her friends, like myself, may oblige with snippets of gossip. All right she can then feed on these, use these to make character sketches of us to be later distorted and incorporated in her books. But to call herself a writer – what a nerve! I must say though, at the end of the day, who cares anyway! Let her taste a dose of her own medicine!

Your friend, Lulú, has already confronted her, saying that if she should recognise in her book so much as a matching eyebrow, she will take her to court and utterly ruin her for the cheap gossip that she is.

As Matilde now lives behind closed doors fearing for her life, no one ever gets to see her. She stays at home Fabiola of Belgium style. As though she weren't unpopular enough, many's the bitching tongue which condemns her as prissy: she only needs to be contaminated, they say, by cigarette paper, and she's off to have a shower.

My arrangement with Mati is that I act as double agent: when I'm at hers I bitch about other friends, and when her back's turned, I bitch about her. It's a 'bitch's circle'! She's well aware of it, however, and claims she doesn't care. I don't know how she finds out about the sniping but she says she loves it.

"I don't care whether they talk ill of me, so long as they talk!"

"Let them say what they like," she says with bitter bravado, "the more the merrier!"

I think you'd love to read *Maria Luján's Belated Revenge*, which won her last year's Centenary of the Pen prize. The novel looks closely at the theme of the gay sensibility in the arts. It's an examination of the origins of an aesthetic which others claim has filtered down to the masses, influencing the public at large and ultimately determining their behaviour. Of course, the gay sensibility thesis is currently the most debated and Matilde herself argues against it. This is the very motive behind her writing the trilogy. *The Decline Of The Electronic Queen* (the subtitle for her 400-page wodge) is followed by *Isa Pròleg's Insurrection*, finishing up with *Queens Of The World, When Will Victory Be Yours*? These novels subscribe to a reactionary and anti-Marxist thesis whereby what queens really desire, as an oppressed and marginal minority, is the 'safeguard' of a moderate Fascism – such as Franco's – because she believes that we have never been treated better than under his regime. She believes that, in a way, a mild reign of terror is the best form of guarantee against our politicisation (exploited as we might easily be by activists and left-wing ideologues!) and against our conversion to Communist guerilladom. Once blinded as we would be by the hype of International Communism, we would one day wake up to the aftermath of glorious 'revolution'. Yes we would discover the terrible reality of our true humiliation – no need to look further than the most renowned cases of Russian and Cuban intolerance, Mati suggests! Moreover, and in her opinion, of course, the very concept of a gay guerilla, no matter how elegantly she be dressed in Yves Saint-Laurent, would be an affront to the sacred dictates of fashion, indeed an insult to haute couture.

As you'll have gathered, thematically, Mati couldn't be more one-tracked. When she presented her college dissertation at University, opinion was firmly divided. Her treatise dealt in fastidious detail with the changing influences of cosmetics and aesthetics on homosexuals and their images down the ages. When it came to 'The Delights Of Nina Ricci', professors polarised into two warring factions. While there were those who would have awarded her the Cum Laude, others clamoured to have her locked up for life in Charenton. As you can see it is Mati, not her subjects, who warrants a case history and it doesn't surprise me that she should spend all day shut away at home. She's frightened to death that she may fall victim to a terrorist attack no doubt dealt by one of those anarchist groups she has it in for politically. But if the truth be known, her ideological distaste for them is none other than the most egotistical paranoia. Her persecution mania is such that she fears for her life – and someone has to be the aggressor.

But Mati has nothing to fear. She is very highly respected on an international level. Intellectuals from all countries come to see her. One afternoon, not long ago, some Argentinian exiles came all the way to see her. But the pilgrimage turned sour and I witnessed a row which was as ridiculous as it was funny.

The Argentinians said what if they had been deported from Argentina..? What of the *desaparecidos*? What if Argentina wasn't so bad a country and...what if..? Matilde, cutting them short, said: "We've done very well out of it for the last forty years with Franco. So have you with your regimes. So for God's sake don't cry for Argentina!"

The Argentinians, outraged, jumped as if they'd had rockets go off under their arses, shouting "You're more of a Fascist than Eva Peron... You've no right to say that...You're not an intellectual... You're phoney...!". With that, the now hysterical Argentinians got up, declaring that they'd be back with a bomb which they'd let off in her face – personally, though, I can't see why they should bother giving her a second thought.

As Matilde has been, as she sees it, Franco's heroine, that's to say, self-appointed Mistress of Progress, she couldn't be prouder. But, in her infinite wisdom, she knows only too well that there's a limit to her brand of heroism. It's no good being sincere or concerned for democracy these days, she says. Who knows what fickle twists fate might hold for her; indeed who knows when the tide will turn, when they might drag her to her death – her crucifixion held at the crossing of Pau Street and Vicent Martir as a salutary warning to all those subversive dissidents.

Well, honey, enough of Matilde. I really must leave you now. As a matter of fact, I've arranged to meet Mati for a bit of mutual mockery and I don't like being late.

If you're interested in Mati's right-wing heresies, let me know, and I'll send you copies. Love from your friend who always has a place for you in her thoughts.

The Adventuress of Macao

LETTER 8
To Aurelio Santonja from Pitita Riutort
Valencia, September 20th, 1975

Darling Aurelio,

On the day of Our Lady of Sorrows, patron Virgin of us unmarried girls, the morning broke with such magnificent, summer sunshine that all our friends got dressed in their late summer clothes, their straw hats, their Ibizan bonnets. So mild was our Indian summer that we decided to go to Vila Ploma on safari. Of course, the construction site workers nearby came down in their lunch break for a blow job among the pine trees. In the hot sun by the sea we made ourselves a paella which we had with gallons of sangria. As the afternoon drew on, we went and sat on the Café Borinot's darling little terrace, to watch the procession of Our Lady of Sorrows, such is our devotion to her.

It was such a gloriously sunlit afternoon: although the day was past its prime, the light gilded the Miquelete monument and Seo pier in all its glorious shades of orange. We were watching the passers-by parading past us, arm in arm, in their Sunday best, their faces and motions spelling boredom, when along comes Tonica Viruelas, who'd arrived from Pego, blowing kisses to each and all of us. We responded with uproarious applause and the most flamboyant of wolf-whistles. She perched beside us, ordered a crème de menthe, saying that the colour matched her emerald earrings – costume ones, of course – and proceeded to enrapture us with one of those fantastic anecdotes that Tonica always brings with her from her hometown.

"Listen, Pepita," she said to me having fixed her black, effervescent eyes on the assembled company, "do you remember that young boy who worked in El Corte Inglés and who used to follow me every evening from seven to nine, no matter where he was supposed to be? Well, you're not going to believe me but I'd just arrived at Pego where I was going to spend a few days with Ramoncín, I drop my luggage, I quickly change into my gorgeous tailored number – you know the one I mean, don't you, Lulú? – the one with the spray of orchids on the skirt and the sun dawning over a Pacific island on the jacket, well, anyway, I'd changed and I was walking down the high street when who do I bump into face to face, grinning from ear to ear... but *him*!"

Oh dear, I was so confused I didn't know whether to cry, biff him one, make off or jump into his arms and devour him whole! He's so handsome, hunky, reckless – with that meanest of matchless smiles. He's got a Robert Redford jaw, defined and square and his tight jeans containing the biggest packet (to use inches would be quite an inadequate measure!). Lulú, he's absolutely custom-made for me!

"Is something the matter?" But as I said so my mind went back to Ramoncín. What a nightmare – the two of them in the same town. This could turn out to be my Waterloo if I didn't watch my step. I had such a shock! And I could literally hear Ramoncín, who's always so attentive, reacting, so jealous is he in his ardent monogamy. But you know, Pitita, I'm the person he needs most. In fact, he's had his fair share. There's no more I can give him after all the care and attention I've lavished. I spent a good six months pampering him morning, noon and night. And all those long impassioned nights spent beating his dick or, should I say, performing our *comédie d'amour*.

And so it was. I decided there and then what to do. Lulú, you must know me by now. Needless to say I went off with my photolove hero, my heartthrob, Corín Tellado.

My agreeing to elope unleashed the beast in Corín. He grabbed me and bit my mouth ferociously – right in the middle of the street! You know how backward the village folk are. Well, you should have seen the looks of an entire family as they watched us from their balcony. Their mouths were agape. I took out my tits. OK, they're not very attractive, but they're still pert and Corín attacked them, biting them and mauling them. Lulú, I was in seventh heaven!

Coming down to earth again, however, the question of loyalty reaffirmed itself. What should I do? Swear allegiance to my new squire, to this man who until now I'd spurned, but who was now suddenly firing on all cylinders, promising to sweep me off to paradise regained. I was in such a state.

But then came what was a blessing in disguise. In a moment of high drama, I suddenly saw Ramoncín and Corín, face to face, bracing themselves to die. It looked as though they'd either fight over me or kill me. I can just see Ramoncín grabbing me by the waist, ruining my favourite suit, and Corín his face long and pale as a basilisk, his eyes looking at me lugubrious and supplicant. Then, freeing myself of Ramoncín, I said to them, "Come on boys, why don't we settle the matter reasonably."

I must have been mad. The last thing I remember happening was seeing them both disappear in a cloud of smoke, the two locked in mortal combat!

Butterfly Songstress was beside herself with laughter – she's never understood how tragic affairs of the heart can be. How could she begin to understand the conflict of our friend's Solomon-style dilemma?

The Naked Countess appeared for a second, her feet full of blue and bruised wounds, only to disappear as swiftly behind the Dolorosa's procession.

Quiriquibú, a Catalan girl who hardly understands a word of the Mass, was dying of laughter, her ears covered, her incredulous voice repeating over and over again, "I don't believe a word of it!" Lulú, on the other hand, looked seriously at her, pressing the point. "So, what did you decide to do with her then?"

But, taking a sip of bitter Campari and, with a feigned giggle, she disappeared into the crowd, under the shower of rose petals which people were throwing over Our Lady of Sorrows. Aurelio, it looks like you and I will be forever spinsters!

You see, nothing changes here: same old friends, parties, springs, summers, autumns, winters – the stuff of provincial living. Above all, imagination is glaringly conspicuous by its absence.

Write soon, Aurelio, we all think of you.
Love from Pitita

To Aurelio Santonja from Lulú Bon
El Puig, September 22nd, 1975

Dear Aurelio,

We've been days preparing for this. I wish you were here, at this country estate, with its smell of orange blossom, its lush green leaves, its enchanted atmosphere and its sky sparkling with distant white clouds.

To walk around this beautiful garden which Loli has created (you know how much money her parents left her), is to have your eyes opened to the injustices of this world. Having chosen to build on high ground her Neoclassical manor, hewn out of the ground, now stands finished and its steps and balustrades are crowned with appropriately period sculptures. Surrounding it are bowers, flower beds, grottoes, waterfalls, swimming pools and flowers, flowers everywhere; in short an idyll which makes you seethe with envy. I couldn't possibly go into every detail, there's so much to describe – a terrible failing considering that without description of detail the place will never come alive. The place conjures infinite sensations and emotions which the profligate Loli, Evil personified, extravagantly evokes, the better to inspire our jealousy.

Each room in the manor is charged with a different smell. If it's not the smell of sandalwood, it's the scent of an incense or amber so intense that your swollen nostrils feel as if they'll explode.

No need to insist on what you already know but bad taste is something which, in Loli, is matched only by her wealth: in both cases OTT. Even that's an understatement. Tawdrier things are to come, so wait for it! The castle/palace/manor is an imitation of a late, a very recent, neo-neo-Neoclassical style, a kind of sub Art Deco. A tower rises solemnly, a mock Miquelet, complete with belltower.

But Loli was not so easily satisfied. Yellow, purple, lilac brocades festoon it, wreathe it from top to bottom, a confection only King Solomon might have dreamt of. From afar it stands ridiculous as a giant tropical bird, crowned as it is by five or six plumes, its coup de grace, which quiver in the evening breeze. In short, like all bombast posing as art, it looks more like a Christmas tree than its ancient architectural model. The ground plan is supposed to take after something quaint and rustic (or so she intended), but she so drowned it in stucco that its initial style has been swamped not to say obscured. The main entrance (one of many!) is made of very solid wood in which the figures of two naked men have been carved. Originally inspired by those on the gates to the palace of the Marques de Dos Aguas, these figures – noblesse oblige! – have since been taken to a beauty parlour, only to return made up to the nines, the toenails on one painted gold, those on the other silver, their eyes bronze, their lips coated with Helena Rubinstein's Deep Lipstick Tender, their eyelids shaded with that blue so popularised by Princess Grace and her daughter Caroline.

My first instinct is to go down to the garden. I think it's still too early to make my entrance and anyway I wouldn't want to have to faint with amazement and have a friend fan me and give me smelling salts to bring me round. My gait, like a queen's as I walk down the stairs, assumes with each delicate descent that air of importance the occasion befits. Before me, on the edges of the path that leads to the house, she has planted magnolias and palm trees. In order to transport and plant them I'm convinced she must have needed to use a bulldozer and cranes, not to mention fifty labourers working day and night.

Loli-Cock will always be true to her name however much her new status has gone to her head. In fact, she paid homage to her name by mucking in with the truckers who delivered and planted her garden. The labourers spent *months* planting trees during which time Loli became progressively more louche and seductive. Whenever we saw her after she'd been busy at the village, her legs splayed like a strutting cowboy as if prized apart by a wedge lodged between them, we'd ask her: "Hi, honey! When will it all be ready?" She'd smile back sarcastically, drink up her crème de menthe and leave the bar where we'd all been sitting.

Now I've seen it I realise how much work and what an ordeal it must have been for her to have it got all ready in time for the autumn. Her estate has two hundred acres worth of orange trees that are a pleasure to behold. A huge garden wall surrounds them lined with godless cypresses – no doubt excommunicated from a cemetery for her to have had enough to plant! At the end of the estate a hillock made of limestone and a coral coloured rock glows gold in the light of day. A waterfall, too, hangs like a fine thread of lace. There's also a grotto full of plastic stalactites and stalagmites sophisticated in its tones of subtle beige and caramel and a subterranean river – that rises up through the ground and trips over it to form a waterfall where a gondola and Italian gondolier are to be seen, the gondolier dressed up in a Venetian T-shirt of blue and white stripes. A stereo sound system plays Claudio Vila's version of *Torna A Sorrento* over and over again, non-stop, like an overwound musical box, the reason being that the silly creature is so enraptured by King Ludwig of Bavaria that she wanted a replica of his famous grotto, asking also that its design make references to the stage of the Opera, Vinatea. Thus inspired, she commissioned the painters at Milan's Scala. But as they were forced to stay there because of some strikes or other, she finally had to contract local artisans who, I think anyway, have produced something much more in Loli's taste. Doubtless divine King Ludwig would have considered the result a masterpiece.

But Loli's real tour de force are her arbours, flowerbeds and fountains which recreate the Valencian style at its most authentic. Do you remember that really old-fashioned landscape gardening at the Viveros Palace with its decadent fountains of slippery algae, brightly coloured goldfish, water-lilies and buttercups? The statuesque white swans and, in the middle, the satyr, holding its huge phallus in its hands as if he were jacking off, a white jet emanating from it.

I've made a count of the fountains: twenty in all, and they've each got their accompanying variegated bed of vibrant flowers. In one vivid bed gloxinias and marigolds catch the eye in the foreground while oleanders form a mellow background. In the middle are hydrangeas with bulbous blooms varying in colour from mauve to violet to light pink – and a sinuous, S-shaped arrangement of yellow tulips.

In another flowerbed the choice of flowers is more exotic still. Antirrhinums, tiny, motley anemones and sombre amarontos are in contrast to a flamboyant row of irises, tiger lilies and African violets which, beside the elegant neutrality of narcissi, vie for aesthetic attention. Half obscured by a clump of reeds, a cherub gambols playfully beside two tiny deer. Lita Vermilion and Lady Washingtona, both from the same town, near Puzol, can be seen constantly running around climbing miniature roses, plucking blossoms and decking their hair with petals, weaving them into their hair and girding their waists with garlands – madcap queens the two of them. Now night is beginning to fall they're sitting on the ground, still weaving together branch after branch of jasmine.

Lita, like the goddess Flora, has deftly strewn her body with the lacy patterns of flowers: a human carpet of floral arabesques, her skin is quite invisible from so much decoration. Lady Washingtona, meanwhile, flushed pink and rotund as a Rubens nymph, gives Lita jubilant chase, pursuing her hotly from arbour to arbour. Naked, in a lake of cobalt blue, they splash about like dolls glimpsed in a child's paradise.

Loli, bewitched by the sight of these athletic creatures, looks on quietly contented, watching as they frolic amongst the iridescent fish. These, visible from afar, testify to the clarity of the water in which Lita and Washingtona duck and dive: its gentle ripples break quietly in a scene otherwise still as a Hockney composition. *Luxe, calme et volupté.*

From the top of the hill, which is surrounded by olive and carob trees with trunks blackened by time, can be seen a magnificent reproduction of the Erecteon, which to all accounts is as authentic as its Greek predecessor. Its facade is caked with different pigments, its columns a salmon pink, its pediment decorated with figures brazenly naked, and painted in an entire tonal range from warm reds, pinks, maroons, oranges to burnt Siena, pillar-box red, all colours finally muddying to darker earth shades. Aloft, the spectacular and watchful figure of Athena. But we're not talking the conventional Greek Athena here: Loli has taken it upon herself to change her into a transvestite, crowning her with the crown and tin radii of Our Lady of the Helpless as well as making her show a leg through the pleats of her folkloric dress! It had never occurred to me how similar the dress of the typical Valencian workman might be to that of the ancient Greeks! The interior of the temple houses a dining room with a marble table and a stone bench for summer dinner parties and banquets. From the top of the hill you can see the fields of orange trees, Loli's mansion and river-cum-lake, which runs through the landscape like the rivers of a Renaissance painting, nostalgic, mythical but now brutally endangered by Loli's squandering of natural resources.

Now that the sun has finally disappeared behind the horizon, it's time to go back inside. A breeze is blowing and it's too chilly to be outside without a shawl or cardy.

Indoors, great commotion. Everyone is busying themselves with the preparations for the evening's soirée, attending, with the elegance of angels, to its many finishing touches. Vases are filled with flowers, ubiquitous candles lit until the hall resembles our Basilica of the Virgin Mary and trays of mouthwatering delicacies are being moved from one table to another (delicacies so delicious that I'd love to put my letter aside and pounce on them!).

The Valencian style cottage which I was telling you about before has been converted into the Palace of the Duke and Duchess of Parcent, so elaborately decorated is it with stucco, niches and Neoclassical alcoves. It's crammed to bursting-point with sculptures and statues, laden with the heaviest curtains of burgundy velvet covering curtains and the carved wood of stately furniture, still exuding the pungent smell of polish. The main reception room's walls are of stucco stippled a honey shade, decorated with an extravagant taste far exceeding the most voluminous Rococo fantasies, giving rise to a suffocating sense of claustrophobia. This in contrast to the austere purism of the Neoclassical staircase which, lightly undulating like the movement of a delicate wave, is fronted with a balustrade whose Baroque magnificence is aesthetically most pleasing. The dining room is bordered by a skirting board of Manises mosaic. This, beside the Mannerism of so much Rococo, lends the room an informality at the same time homely, relaxing and elegant; complementary, too, to the handsome Italian style of the decor as a whole with its pastel drawings in a decorative and impressionistic style. Hanging in the passage is an extravagantly embroidered Manila tapestry, a present from the Phillipines, brought back by her mother, before she was killed in a car crash. Loli is still mourning the death of Doña Soledad, her mother, the scar still unhealed.

But I think what would really impress you above all, Loli's monstrosities aside, are the *human* lamps and candelabra which stand, clad merely in the most transparent muslin, on stylised pedestals of pink alabaster. These evoke King Solomon's columns at their most sophisticated and refined. To watch them brush against each other with their voluptuous and delicate agility is to imagine fantasies beyond the dreams of the most decadent Roman emperors!

As Loli's friends arrived, aghast and awe-struck by the sheer luxury and splendour of her creation, they were dumbfounded at the aphrodisiacs before them – men supernaturally endowed, muscle and marble mixing. A Tower of Babel formed by tier upon tier of plumes, quivered under a giant fan. Half-muffled cries of admiration circulated with the speed and impact of an echo heard inside a mountain on the verge of eruption.

Everyone wanted to tickle the groins of the lamp-men, provocatively finger their navels or measure the proportions of their dicks. No matter how flaccid they were, an abnormal interest in sizing them up became everyone's obsessive focus of attention.

Loli stood at the top of the staircase relishing the success of her rented slaves, transformed magically into lamps-cum-studs, fantastic ironmongery hired off the streets for a night of lust which would remain forever branded on her guests' memories.

Anyone worthy of note was there. Faces either new or well-known, from all corners of the globe, formed the guest list. There was:

Hostess Loli-Cock
Lita Vermilion

Lady Washingtona
Bolchévique
Jilguera of Aldaya
Momy Von
Cazalla Lil
Songstress
Butterfly
Juke-Box
Hilda of Perelló
Rosita the Pathetic
Pamela Typhoid
L'il Lulú
Hysteria-a-Go-Go
Peppermint
Toia Pudenta Mariquita
López
Visantera Firework
Xorrofum
Quica Quintacolumnista
Mary Sky Stiu
Fallera Orthopaedica
Celia Chinela
Chiffon
Pitita Ruitort
Alicia Falla
Neleta Rebordonida
Maria "O" Queen Juanita
Palmar Leech
Sit on my Arse
Amparo Iturbi
Carmelina Cabalero
Nanci Night
Ranita of Granollers
Marona or English Rose.

Among Valencia's aristocracy, the following Royal Highnesses
were present:

Ruiz of Lyori

Quiriquibú
Matilde Belda
Teresita Rulls
Xona Pérez
Periquita
The Queen of Almenara
Pajillera
Cocktease
Madame Bovary
Rudy Valentina
Liberty Maritime
Encarna Bolillos
Blanca Doble
Allioli (otherwise known as Garlique)
The Adventuress of Macao
Lali Turner
Pipi Yaguer (Thunder Thighs)

(Just interrupting the roll call to say we kept a minute's silence for
the incarcerated Korea – and wept buckets!)

Amparito Rockefeller
Maruja Ironcunt
Vicky Vision
Holier Than Thou Pi (the virgin of Alginet)
Nina Foc
Penélope Tutú
Susi Polvorera
Armchair Gay
Cuenca
Metralleta Mariquita
Lady Hashish
Gorgon
Nazarena
Polola Pérez
Ranglan
Patachoux
F.A.C
Sensurround

Butane
Violet Rascayú
Lola Glamour
Frigid Potens
Pelikan
Virgo Prudens
Piluca of Perpignan
Alexandra of the Lake
The Queen of Chaillot
The Virgin Queen
Acrata Lys
Anarchy Gadé
Just Call Me Eva
Mad Molla
Plumero
Unamuna
Lola Flowers
Paquita Rich
Stunted Calfa
Trini Trujillo
Little Girl Cholek
Mujerona
Panoli
Carlos Besada
Lulú Bon (myself)

– and a host of feather-bearers, party-partying and stuffing their faces with all that Loli's mansion had in the way of hallucinatory delights. After the first few moments of stage fright had passed, everyone began to talk animatedly until the sound of competing voices, increasingly amplified, filled the house with excited noise.

I must leave you now as I can't stop gorging and the party mood is going to my head. I'm being hassled by so many fellow-guests who at every turn pinch my arse. Dressed as Ginger Rogers, my outfit impels me to dance – if I don't start cancaning round the room soon frustration will make me come up in a rash. Besides what would become of me if I couldn't show off my crown of feathers to full advantage? I defy anyone to find a more sumptuous example of my glamorous millinery. Either in the entire Queendom of Valencia or its neighbouring towns and villages!

Tomorrow, or the day after, I'll carry on telling you about the faggotry organised by Loli for this party. I can safely say that it is without precedent, save for the last orgy which took place before the arrival in Valencia of King James I's Catalan troops. Judging by the archives which Loli dug up in the Monastery, the king himself shows every sign of having been a host equal to Loli. From what we can gather from the history books, although he was a conquistador of the most macho and aggressive sort. Yet other sources tell us that it only took him to arrive in Valencia for him to meet up with the local queens and throw caution to the winds.

I've just realised that one extremely butch lamp-man is giving me the louchest eye. I must be off but as you are so good a friend I've decided to dedicate him to you! Physically he is mine, but in spirit he will be yours. Tonight looks like being a night to remember.

Lulú (The mirror crack'd from side to side, The curse is on me cried!...)

LETTER 10
To Aurelio Santonja to Lulú Bon
El Puig, 25th September, 1975

My dearest Aurelio,

Everyone's lost track of how long this party's been going. I'm
writing to you during one of its moments of respite, that is
between one meal and another. Or should I say between one fuck
and the next. As you can imagine everyone's quite disorientated.
If this carries on it really must be because God wills it! Or because
Loli, tactician that she is, plots and plans that her ball be the belle
of them all!

But I think that by now the party's on its last legs. People are
throwing up everywhere. The house, which I've described to
you before in the greatest detail, is now a sorry dump; more to the
point a sewer, after what we've been up to. If only you could see
Momy Von over there, pissed as a newt – and looking like one,
being virtually on all fours. Bottle of whisky in hand, she's fairly
knocking it back and every sip misses her mouth. She's
precariously perched on the most exquisite velvet chairs, now
riddled with cigarette burns and stains that have quite ruined the
fabric as it hangs in shocking tatters. The place looks like a
municipal rubbish dump!

I can scarcely explain to you just what a shambles this place
is in – and that's when my head isn't spinning! I've tried everything, alka seltzers, the lot, but to no avail. But I will try to
be objective about it. Everyone, apart from the indefatigable
Momy Von, of course, are asleep in their rooms. So the house
is quite deserted. Dawn is bringing with it a buzz of outside activity: a few chickens have come into the house,

rummaging about on the floor amongst so much food gone to waste...

This letter is in reply to your first one. As for your repulsive friend, Eugenio, I've got nothing to say about him at the moment. If he doesn't write to you, I suppose he'll say that he caught got up in one of those rackets he's so fond of. But I will try to find out what I can and let you know in my next letter.

I've also got the cassettes sitting on my desk but you can't make anything out. Just this constant cacophony. So I'll try to give you an idea of everything that's happened here, in writing. There's so much to tell you, although, as you know, my powers of concentration are on the blink. I think that the last time I wrote to you was when the human 'lanterns' made their memorable entrance. Us queens shrieked in unison over and over again, jumping with joy at Loli's flamboyant ingenuity. We all *knew* that Loli had more than just one surprise in store for us. But we had no idea just how many! Firstly, at Loli's bidding, the lanterns, crowned with lighted candles, approached us, in a perfect formation of balletic majesty. Aurelio, just imagine us watching them stepping down from their pedestals with those bodies covered only in diaphanous gauze, jacknives and combs strapped to their garters – it was more than anyone could bear! (I defy you to name one person who hasn't thrilled at the thought of a man armed with a knife all of a dark night!) Everyone was falling off their seats, shouting and whistling like hysterical schoolkids, hoping that those voluptuous figures might turn us all into women, and I mean WOMEN!

The theatre had begun: Loli clicked her fingers and out came the knives. There was a general hush of fear mixed with awe. The boys struck an identical pose and stopped. (In the meantime, we were still inanely and absentmindedly smoothing our skirts!)

Then, clicking open their knives and coming forward with a cruel curl of the lip, they ripped open their clothes, buttons and fastenings flying. Nylon briefs, scarlet and striptease artist black stockings, raced through the air. True, these guys were well-paid professionals. But all the same they worked together with an amazing enthusiasm, as if galvanised into action out of pride for their work. Apart from the obvious fact that they were being encouraged by the general shindy of us excitable queens, I couldn't work out how they mustered such an impressively athletic act.

No doubt about it – Loli had hired the best boys you could hope to find.

In moments, their clothes of sheerest muslin had slipped away. And when they bared their muscles, a wild and explosive cry swept every corridor and room in the house. In any other circumstances this would have sounded like a portent of the blackest atrocities. Suddenly there was a silence!

Remember those nightmarish movies of advancing zombies? Those wakeful dead who struck anyone who crossed their paths dumb? That's how it felt. However free we were with the champagne, our tongues stayed parched, rough as sandpaper. You should have seen the tension on everyone's faces – turmoil and fear, fright and longing indissolubly mixed. The *zombies*, arranged in rows of five, were like soldiers in conquest of virgin lands or in this case, of bodies apprehensive of the pleasure which violence inspires. Again they stopped, their faces deadpan. From the corner of my eye, I could see how everyone was deviously trying to will over to him the man who most caught his fancy. In Machiavellian fashion they wove in and out of each other, pretending to ignore what was going on.

Jilguera of Aldaya, herself, couldn't believe what she saw, even though one monster, of colossal proportions, and lusciously equipped, was homing in on her. But to us it was clear as day that he would impale her, pulp her innards like a food mixer. The blade had pounced but Jilguera still played dumb.

Then, finally realising that fiction was indeed fact, Jilguera began to sigh a long deep sigh followed by a supplicant, "Fuck me! Fuck me!" It only took him to reach out for her to start stroking his strapping cock. She mustered a hitherto latent strength and, earnest as a virgin, attended to his cock. "I'm going to eat it whole!" she said, "I'm going to take it! My God, what balls!" And she tossed him off, drawing from him every crystalline drop, gingerly licking the trickling juices from his *cornucopia* as if she were licking at a strawberry ice cream.

The giant *lantern* lifted her on her axes and, in a thrice, had her naked and trembling. Then, thrusting her up and flipping her over, he pawed her cruelly, like a cat plays with its prey before finally bearing down on it.

Like a fragile bird to that colossal, resplendent body, Jilguera could be heard warbling with pleasure and longing for that cock, which now tantalisingly near, now frustratingly far, looked as if it would finally get down to action and do the deed once and for all.

To encourage it, she shifted from side to side, like a broody hen, positioning herself for action. Meanwhile, the manipulative bastard deliberately deprived her of the pleasure, relentlessly pulling away from her as quickly as he lunged. While he laughed, Jilguera cried with rage, "Just you wait, fucker, once it's in, it's mine for good!"

Operation Crisco was underway. The sound effects of sex had begun in earnest. Loli, standing at the top of the staircase, like a priest on his pulpit, looked on ecstatic. At the touch of a switch, the room was darkened and a huge cloth, which until then had enigmatically covered one of the walls, began to lower itself gradually.

With our attention on Lulú, everyone's sexual antics came to a halt – we were frozen into a sexual *tableau vivant*. We looked up and there was Loli, sitting resplendent in a dress of alpaca, festooned with cultured pearls, a garland of petunias in her lap. On her sultry face, gentleness and cruelty, naiveté and coquettishness mingled as she sat beneath a royal canopy on a landing decorated with drapes of peacock blue damask, culminating in a gold, tasselled fringe, a tester fronted with a crest describing the insignia of 'Centenary of the Pen!' – and crowning it, a plume.

We might all be queens we agreed, but it was she who reigned over Puig. This we immediately and tacitly acknowledged – our silent unanimity was none other than a coronation by consensus. "She's like the Empress of Sissi, herself!" whispered one person, "she ought to appear in *Hello!* Such majesty!"

"She's more than just a queen, she's a *lady* – look, if it's not Joan Crawford coming down the stairs of her bar, playing Vienna, in her tight trousers and boots, her swashbuckling ruffled shirt and wild curly hair. Such confidence, such aplomb!"

The cloth was still falling and the lights of a huge neon were flashing rhythmically on and off. We heard, in stereo, the sound of *Els Segadors*, set to Rudi Venturi's cha-cha-cha rhythm. Sex petered out as we covered ourselves in whatever was at hand, curtains, underwear, pillows. For our anthem had begun. Excitedly we joined in, our arms raised. Whenever the lights flashed on we caught glimpses of ourselves and could see our skin bristling with goose pimples.

Suddenly, there was silence – everyone was gripped with awe. From the wall, where the cloth had been, we saw a shining, flashing screen from which emerged a gigantic pin-ball machine, its handles exquisitely tooled in the shape of phalluses. Inside the machine, the holes down which the balls normally fall were designed to resemble open arseholes. But their wit didn't stop there. Whenever a ball dropped down one, lights flashed on the board and the sign, "1,000 points. Fuck me!" would be suddenly illuminated.

This was the sacking of Troy all over again! We all jumped on to it and played: and, of course, every time someone scored 1,000 points they'd be fucked. If the score was a 10,000 the reward was blow-job and so on.

This was the *Fuck Poker* we had all fantasised about at some time as repressed children. Now, Loli, Lady Phallus, had given us more than we could have ever dreamed of.

Our thanks to you then, Loli! We'll never forget what you did for us provincial Valencianitos, normally bored out of our tiny minds. Valencia: a city more uneventful there could not be.

Aurelio, I couldn't tell you how long the orgy lasted. Alcohol, sex, all kinds of excesses dissipated all sense of space and time. Writing to you now, at dawn, I think to myself how wonderful it would be to live only as long as it took these seemingly endless festivities to burn themselves out.

But fate will no doubt play one of its nasty turns on us. There'll be some price to pay for all of this. Poor provincials that we are! Goodbye, Aurelio. Who knows what tomorrow will bring? I only wish you were here! At least we're in the same boat, the same downward spiral, whether we're separated or not.

Forever yours,
Lulú

LETTER 11
To Aurelio Santonja from Lulú Bon
El Puig, 28th September, 1975

"Fill your heart and love today," Juke-box sang to Jilguera of Aldaya thereby causing the red light of her secret sexual machinery to spark into action.

Jilguera's singing was a phenomenon to be avoided: the nearest queens began to flap about, some of them probably tripping up as they fled. Among them Hilda del Perello, parcelled and tightly packed in a racing green dress of smooth *crêpe de chine*, three pleats and a black flower cinching her waist.

The panic had made her lose a heel off her shoe and a cigarette holder of *or maché* which her mother had given her when she was sent off to a debutantes ball at the Yachting Club.

Her consternation, however, was nothing compared to Teutonic Momy Von Kane's the moment she discovered a rip in the train of her floaty organdie dress which she now trailed behind her with feigned indifference. Panic was to be avoided at all costs. Who knows what damage it might do to the outfit in question? "Bastards!" she muttered without stopping to take breath, causing a smiling Songstress Butterfly to cackle so much that she desperately tried to contain the convulsions of her swollen belly. But to no avail: such were her convulsions that she watched in horror as a false eyebrow fell into her glass of whisky. A circle of people gathered round. Simply Electric appeared with a 100 per cent cotton jockstrap and the cackling Butterfly Songstress bawdily sang "So prominent a prick, so large and thick!"

Virgo Prudens, however, was oblivious to such mirth. Lying in a sea-shaped shell, like Venus herself, and suspended more than a metre up in the air, she slept unmoved. She was wrapped in the densest dream, a transparent curtain of frosted glass fronting

49

the shell which atomised the amber glow of the room into thousands of dancing, dazzling points of light. But neither the bustle of the party nor its clamour would awake her.

The others wouldn't hear of it: to think that the willpower of the entire room was being called upon to prize this sleeping mollusc out of its hermetic bed, anyone would think that she was being brought to justice! "You just can't get a moment's rest," said Alexandra Lake with mock sympathy, only too aware of Virgo's imminent deflowering! Meanwhile, to add to Jilguera's cacophonous attempts at singing, there was further commotion with the competitive and near violent jostling of feathered headdresses.

Virgo couldn't be left alone: suddenly down she came couch and all. A thundering din was heard, followed by two queens fainting over the wreckage just as the hysterical squeals of Juke-Box reverberated round the main reception room. Its wall to wall gilt, its walls again embossed with amber and gold, and, where these met the ceiling, a honey-coloured satin, studded with a band of emeralds were a sight to behold – indeed a typical reproduction Valencian town hall. But these paled into lacklustre insignificance beside Juke-Box's caterwauling.

Chaos apart, competition began to escalate. A well-timed faint is a victory won twice over, a tactic so beknown to us that it has become a refrain. Hence the lack of chairs, sofas, chaises longues etc. on which we queens could fall and swoon with artistic aplomb.

The war was on – us queens were vying for attention and nothing was going to stop us now. Only a few survivors would make it to the table with its immaculate cloth of white broderie anglaise, its platinum cutlery, its delicacies and victuals whose variety defy description. But, Aurelio, before you wonder how any of us could possibly think of eating I can assure you we were all famished!

For the end of the evening everyone was dressed up in some manner or other. A costume change had been reserved for the grand finale. Polola Perez, one queen who appeared in the papers as a pioneer of some endless range of cosmetics (thus earning her the universal nickname Queen Cosmetica) had dressed up in a vinyl costume. Her inspiration? Dale Arden, in the film, *Mongo*, in which he is chased by the most beautiful *batmen*. But if the truth be known, however, she really looked more like a deep-sea diver than anything else.

F.A.C meanwhile grandly stood with her back to the huge mirror which dominated the dining room and thus delivered forth to the gathering at large a farewell speech.

"Beloved queens from all parts of Valencia. This reunion is comparable only, in its numbers and its success, to the assembly of hunchbacked virgins who last year met in Lourdes. Fellowship makes for strength, a strength delicate and divine. Gathered together like this our strength exceeds that of the air force... indeed we are," (She actually said this.) "a giant aerodynamic plume conquering the frontiers of liberty."

A standing ovation followed, a wave of sighs of admiration, a shower of white and coloured feathers to mark a historic, if brief, speech. And so did the reunion, held this year by Loli in Puig, conclude itself. Half dead we rolled out of the grand mansion, assured that we had won a war – and if not a war an important strategic battle.

A long line of cars made for the motorway turning to Pucol. Thus we dispersed, each to her own town. Farewells were said, kisses given, words exchanged about how much we looked forward to seeing each other at next year's AGM.

Best wishes from a friend who, it has to be said, is feeling slightly worse for wear,

Lulú

Dearest Aurelio,

I believe I owe you a rational explanation for recent goings on, knowing full well that the news that would have reached you will have been distorted and manipulated by a sensationalist press, not to say passed on as rumours by those who are ignorant of what really happened.

No need to set the record straight on the press cuttings which as I gathered from your letter you've already seen. Lulú, too, with her characteristic folly, has put together a photo-novel on the subject, which I'm sure will give her no end of fodder for future gossip.

Many bigwigs are embroiled in a case but when they are called to bear witness they cravenly pass the buck. The witch hunters are after their pound of flesh, I just know it! They have me at their mercy and one of those who 'could' have given favourable evidence has died. The assumption that I was the murderer is considered a foregone conclusion, yet the police have no corroborating proof.

The prison is dank and my despairing letter, written with a stump of a pencil, is steeped in sadness. Who could possibly want to die of love in the manner of Lulú's tragic fiction? Her message is not mine – I want to live whatever happens!

My family have been dropping me one by one. From what I hear my mother is the only one to besiege the prison walls and proclaim my innocence wherever she goes. I'm innocent and I want you to know that.

I've been here for two months now and the lawyers have been trying to catch me out with their specious formulae, which at the hour of trial would be no good to me. Everyone wants to destroy me. All those respectable people, those models of society are just a load of shits. But of course it's not in my interest to name any names.

In case you didn't know, my job was simply to take down the details of the blokes I was recruiting outside the town. We simply took them there and that was all. When I informed the police about the men on the estate, they found nothing. The owner, a man as respectable as he was sinister, told me that he would not take out any official charges against me, due to the consequences, nor would he claim any damages.

And what about the guys I can hear you ask? They disappeared, vanished into the night. After the police took down the christian names of the men I'd known, in the enquiry they made, they couldn't track them down. The others, I'm sure, have disappeared off the scene, probably paid to do so by the very people who'd employed them in the first place.

Everything points to the incident being a lot uglier than either Andres or I thought. It was Andres who was far more embroiled than I in this set-up. They had him under their thumb all right. He's taken all he knew to the grave with him. And Andres' lover? They found out that he's been travelling abroad for two months on a false passport that gives him entry to Spain, France, England. It's a cliché, I know, but with money you can buy anything! Anyway, I've got two aces up my sleeve which, as you can guess, I can't divulge. Security at the prison is tight and I have to be very careful that they don't find out.

For the time being, this is all I can tell you. You know how much I love you and I hope you will understand my desperate position. In the meantime, your entertaining letters always cheer me up!

Lots of love from your friend, Pepe

P.S. You know I'd never have killed Andres. I loved him so much! Here, in prison, I miss him all the more.

LETTER 13
To Aurelio Santonja from Lulú Bon and Carlos Besada
Valencia, 30th September, 1975.

Dear Aurelio,

I've got painful news, and although I don't like to tell you, I feel it's my duty. Eugenio has been taken to the emergency unit at the clinic. His body is riddled with knife wounds and his condition is critical.

I know how much you loved Eugenio. But with the life he was leading recently – I don't know whether you're aware of this – but, anyway, no one was surprised by what happened. We know only too well what Eugenio was like. His gradual loss of sanity had become common knowledge. You've probably heard about the friends that he went around with and the ridiculous goings on in town at the time. I think you ought to know that the accident happened in North Station's public toilets. A fight with the legionnaires left him knocked flat inside the toilets, but luckily he wasn't killed. Lulú's gone to the clinic so I'll soon have news from her.

Carlos Besada

P.S. Aurelio, Eugenio is having an operation, although a friend of mine told me that when he went into the clinic he was breathing so poorly that they'd given him up for dead. We won't know anything for certain until the morning. His family have deserted him and didn't want to tell me anything more. I hope his friend calls me. In any case I'll send you a telegram tomorrow if I can give you an update. Apparently one of the knife wounds has affected him so badly that as a result of the shock he is now suffering from a brain haemorrhage. I'll try to keep you informed and I'll do anything I can to help.

With lots of love, Lulú.

(NEWS CUTTING OF THE EVENTS)

Valencia. *Brawl in public toilets. According to police sources, at 00.35 last night the body of 28-year-old Valencian E.M.R. was found. He was critically wounded in the toilets of the Railway Station to the north of the town.*

The injured man has knife wounds, the deepest being to the victim's rib cage. This damaged a lung, and other wounds were inflicted on his neck, abdomen and left hand. He also has head wounds from his attackers which caused a brain haemorrhage, resulting in a stroke and a coma.

The motives for the attack are as yet unknown but personal revenge has not been ruled out. Of the arrested men, three legionnaires are to be put on trial, once all legal niceties have been seen to.

TELEGRAM
No 01512 Pal 14/7 day 31 Hour... Pesetas...
EUGENIO SAFE, STOP. LONG CONVALESCENCE,
DIFFICULT RECOVERY, STOP. BRAIN INJURY, STOP.
COULD HAVE STROKE, STOP.

"Art is innocent"

"Art is innocent"

Fight all threats to your fate
That would counter its dictates;
Accept as mortal all ambitions
Of eternal glory and artistic visions;
Consider human, not divine
Your aspirations to works sublime.
And why restrict other's lives,
When you allow your whims to thrive?
Villamediana, *Faeton*

I feel free to fail. This was all I had to do – to commit a crime against that airhead – to break the mould of that small-talking society which condemns us to seek victory over it. According to the logic of our society I couldn't help but act self-destructively: the life of excess I want to lead is at loggerheads with *reason*. Excess is condemned for its condemnation of "reason". Repression is a life without Eros and imagination. All cultural and artistic movements which have tried to make the erotic manifest and to incorporate it into everyday life have been suppressed by the many-headed monster of social order. To abandon oneself to excess is to subvert the status quo, moulded by centuries of historical conventions, and turn it upside down, shake it, invert it, give vent to its obscene, raw pornographic potential, indulge in the intimacy of the vulgar – cosmetics, bottles of multicoloured liqueurs, cheap metals, plastics, adverts, tin foil, disposable bakelite, mysterious treasure chests full of hidden objets d'art, crystals, satin, flashing stainless steel, sandwich-board men, soft polyurethane, soft cheeses, scouring pads, unashamedly crude as an empty tin waiting to be filled by abattoir offal. The ultimate revolutions occur, ironically, in the most banal contexts: witness the TV show in which the scrubbed, shiny-as-a-coin face of the compère interacts with the awe struck spectators who as the show progresses find their minds wandering, their subconscious thoughts conjuring unspeakable fantasies, unspeakably private pornographic scenarios, the most far-flung and orgiastic of desires untold.

Shouldn't we make of our bodies living manifestos of sexual fulfilment – manifestos which would flaunt themselves daily, brazen 'banners' of erotic exuberance?

Let's break down the barriers and parameters of a future both stale and sterile in which they would have us mummified.

Pornography is corruption in philosophic form.

Sexual corruption engenders *disruption*.

Funny to think that we are limited to using virtually the same wizened language of the past to express our objectives for the future – as if the language of the past inevitably compromises our future actions. If words are the springboard for action, let's free them from the parochial usage which so infects them, incurably, terminally. Let them express, instead, the gratuitous – more specifically the contingencies of lust. Romantic fiction gives these away, too. Its clichés, ironically, give the lie to a wealth of repressed perversions. Countless tales are told of submission and domination (rose-tinted S & M) material nonetheless for the subversion of social 'standards'.

This is the kind of pornography where pleasure is ambivalently portrayed. Ostensibly in favour of social repression, a seamier content nonetheless escapes.

Why then should anyone be surprised by my

behaviour? None of us are ignorant of how timidly conformist we are as a race. As I see it every opportunity should be taken to savage the stagnant well of our social passivity; to disrupt the spell of anything for a quiet life, that not-in-my-backyard mentality which is so blatantly hypocritical at our expense. Only through inflicting chaos can we fight back: ironically their obscenity meets with what is deemed to be our 'obscenity'. Thus does their ammunition inadvertently feed our arsenals.

Wouldn't you agree that homosexuality is a state of supreme enlightenment?

Those who don't flick through *Elle*, *Diez Minutos*, Garbo or *Hello!* might as well have lost touch with reality, not to say denied themselves the furthest reaches of the imagination. It's precisely appearances – the veneer of glossy magazines – that reveals things to us as they are really are. For what could be more profound than the skin-deep – which, of course, includes us?

Can anything seriously replace metaphor for pure pornography, caprice or delirium? Metaphor, illusion artfully studied, makes us feel richer for fantasy, excess, frivolity, aesthetic pleasure, texture, colour, the movement in photographs – daguerrotypes, which in their impressionism, trigger off a chain of associations. Without Hollywood, too, where would we find the models for our transgression, the inspiration for our constant manipulation of persona?

There is sophistication in subversion through inverted, one might say 'other' desires, and in our tapping of feelings which society has long kept buried. How much better a sky that reeks of brimstone and atmospheric anarchy?

What I want to know is when are we going to admit to our common pride, to our capacity for euphoria in the midst of despair?

No, I'm not cruel, I'm just your metaphor! (...)

Wouldn't it be fair to say that perversity is founded on innocence? (...)

"Didn't you know it's lust's prerogative to destroy love?" (...)

It's as if everyone is desperate to cling to reality, and hold on to it at the price of fantasy. There's too high a premium on losing oneself in fiction – though it always threatens to usurp reality anyway.

Do you remember how intimately you and I came to know the secrets of our desires?

Here I am, writing, thinking of nothing in particular. It's an incredible luxury – it's like being a millionaire, the only way to be. Idleness – it's the only respectable occupation.

So here I am cruising twenty-four hours a day, indulging my desires indiscriminately, tracking down those numb nine-to-fivers, undressing them, fucking them senselessly. That's what I like about it – the fact that it's neither here nor there whether I do so or not, neither vital nor necessary since nothing is necessary much less my capricious and compulsive pursuit of pleasure. But how it obsesses me! Looking back, I left myself open to abuse when, still starved of romance, I took to the streets in a desperate search for love and passion! How things have changed. All I want now is to have sex with a vengeance which means I'm constantly on the prowl. I've lost the romantic spur which once fired my sexual adventures.

Now I'm like an explorer, stranded in the desert, feeling too apathetic, frankly too unwilling to find my way out of it. Which is not to say I'm bored. I *have* taken to my ways! I love the comforts of an indolent life. I've left far behind me now the spontaneity and impulse once responsible for my most outrageous actions. Sex has become a bodily function – and rightly so. It suits me if it's formulaic, devoid of emotion or reckless passion. After all it should simply be a routine – a job. Sex is but the conformity to ritual, the magnetism of the streets. Stable relationships, solid emotional ties only lead to domestic torpor, to a marital deathbed of diplomacy and tedium.

I, for myself, prefer the orgiastic chaos of thoughts which, forever disrupted by desire, cannot be resolved or consummated in their perpetual unrest. Having reasoned my behaviour thus far, I can only conclude that relations are atomic, electric and owe as much to repulsion as to attraction. Desire is best rationalised, made mechanical, turned into a physical schema but one which fractures into hundreds of luminous threads, which liquifies on contact with another's flesh. Flesh which daily nourishes your geiger counter, your physical prowess. It's time we transformed our tedium into a searing laser, destructive, unmitigatedly insane and uncontrollable – subject it all to an infinite pain whose orgy of synaesthesic sensation will utterly defeat all efforts at resistance. The body must be changed back into a machine, complete with its own self-destruct mechanism; be the instigator of change in the face of those who, unwittingly, will arm you with the weaponry of change. (...) We'll never discover our real selves unless we master gesture and mannerism. For gestures perfectly describe and encapsulate appearances (...) We've had to devise our 'performance', invent a persona complete with clothes, make-up and, by extension, new features – which was no mean feat! We've had to be nonentities, going through life unnoticed, anonymous heroes punched out of a mould, carbon copies that no one would think to look at twice.

Questioning appearances may provide us with the means of subverting the values which up until now have deformed us, twisted us, moulded us, misrepresented us in accordance with their own image. (...)

Whenever people said to me, "Fuck me harder!" how I enjoyed doing just that. Indeed, sometimes I felt like tearing them apart, ripping their flesh to pieces and eating it, live and creeping, before their eyes. Savouring my partners would be the only way to make my theories materialise, I thought; I would have stripped them to the core, seen their intestines, smelt their stench as they rotted, fingered their shit and tasted it – a taste exactly equivalent to their facial expression, their terror in the face of my cannibalism. My relish is nothing if not awesomely sophisticated – a pleasure which so many others would like to share if only they'd admit it! Especially those who feel their unhealthy inhibitions fall apart when they think of the moral vicissitudes of their own history – and generally of human history, for after all, both are relatively recent. Like fusing circuits, our electrical relays are forced miraculously into motion: our memories come to life, vivid as most three-dimensional film. It's our secret fear which, tucked away as it is with our carnal desires, invokes them, forces them out of their confines.

Carried away by the magic of words, they burst into action, and, sparks flying, burn everything in their wake, in a reckless, anarchic outburst – so do discipline, willpower, co-ordination and self-control fall instantly by the wayside. There is no turning back – as words acquire their cutting edge, so decorum gives way to lust and abandon, the fear of death to an apprehensive delight in sex. That's why I chose to draw from the language of toilet graffiti, of horoscopes and the dross of provincial papers, of pop lyrics, leaflets, political stickers in an effort to restore language to its historic origins. For such words throw light on the flimsy authority of culture and its constraints, culture that undermines spontaneity and denies the value of myth.

When divorced from the 'mythic' quality of language I felt all sense of history abandon me. It struck me that language was divested of myth and had become excessively cultural and so sterile.

In contrast, my words lifted from adland have a childlike nostalgic ring, redolent of the stirrings of myth: how else could I explain their inarticulate and revitalising quality if not in terms of the bland, plastic surface of a food processor whose amorality as happily would process limbs, brains, ankles, livers, castrate men's cocks, pure blood and onions mixing finally – like processed thought – to produce metaphor.

For years, we have been complicit with sex as a dumb, reproductive function. Now its offspring – its foetuses – are hungering for the mythic, for unfettered poetry, impromptu, taking those who hear it by surprise, restoring to language its mainspring, to metaphor its life, to academic verse its energy, in short ridding it of poetic necrophilia.

In this sense, it was our aim to rejuvenate meaning, to describe every object *authentically*.

Isn't it time you let yourself go, too?

Are you so afraid of what you really want? Why do you run away instead of discovering your fears and exploring them? Instead all you do is repress your naughty desires, rap them on the knuckles like an obedient and self-policing child. But you would do better to throttle your fears and let desire grip you by the loins. Surrender to the gluttony of sex I say! Break with your inhibitions and you'll find happiness. Poetry is but love, love sheer abandon!

> "Many universities have invited me to hold a discussion of ideas with their students, but I systematically refuse to do so on the grounds that universities are not life."
> Linda Lovelace, *Intimate Diaries*

I don't feel in the right frame of mind to be objective. I've never been objective. How love hurts! How my heart aches – alone in the wasteland!

What an absurd paradox, this Fate: this vicious circle of order and chaos!

Today another queen has been murdered. This time the victim was carved up from head to foot like a slab of veal, the bits put in a trunk. I remember her face was made up; from her lips oozed a trickle of white cream.

The night is thick with the chimera of fear! The strangler of Grao strikes again! At dusk Grao is a ghost town. The gay bars close after eleven. The port is empty, reflecting impassively the rosary of coloured lights above and the rippling surface of the sea stirred by the swaying of boats.

Only a lone passer-by, solitary, shrouded in mist, dares to walk the area. The strangler of an ambiguous, vulnerable gender wreaks solitary revenge on the tenderest victims. At daybreak the morning peace is shattered by the screams of lust turned gangrenous.

Not even the memory of daylight can rid us of

our night-time fears – a night full of moribund caresses.

I used to love stroking the surfaces of things. Only by first passing through the pores of their skins can we reach inside them. Today culture is but a cliché, devoid of content.

We wanted to punish so many. We wanted to humiliate and make others bend to our corporal punishment. We carried chains, wore knuckle dusters, leather truncheons and our electric dildo – that essential tool if we were to leave the avenue drenched in spunk and blood – as we so wished... The three of us, dressed in black leather and rubber, our gear flashing silver studs, got off our motor-bikes. Total silence, save for our footsteps.

We stood in position like futuristic marble statues, standing in military formation, our presence giving the otherwise innocent night a certain edge. Gradually, as if ghosts or zombies emerging from a trance, the predators appeared one by one. They cruised us, circling us quietly and stalking us among the flower beds. We brushed past each other, pretending to do so casually. But we were sizing up each other's proportions and vital statistics, a multitude of nocturnal spectres jostling in a patch just a few metres square, as if this was the only space available to us along the massive avenue. Then, at the sound of a revving car, or of advancing *foreign* footsteps, we would suddenly disperse with all that that accompanies – but when peace returned, we would resume our search for the compulsive satisfaction of the senses, the clandestine pursuit of sex.

A boy has just approached *Johnny*. His look is faraway and, as he masturbates Johnny, his body rocks very slightly. Johnny strokes the boy's cock which hangs languidly between them. He leans back to form a hollow at his crotch the better to thrust it forward into the other's leather-hipped pelvis.

I'm being cruised by an old gaffer who's as camp as knickers and who is no doubt attracted to rubber. He takes out his prick. Drawing towards him, I decide to reciprocate and take out my 110 V vibrator to find out what reaction this electric charge will elicit from this body bucking with desire.

What *Micky* likes, and what he has always liked, is to shoot off. He likes to flaunt his cock and offer it to the highest bidder – a lover of casual, outdoor sex. And he always finds someone: leaning against a eucalyptus tree at this moment, his legs apart, he can feel the first warm strokes of an anonymous tongue working on his groin. Doubtless the stranger will do the job required of him, performing with a dexterity gained from experience as well as instinct – sucking, after all, is a function which goes back to childhood! Micky's cock is so sensitive that no sooner has it felt the boy's warm, moist mouth enclose it, his tongue seeking out the hidden subtler erogenous zones of his crotch, than he begins to groan and gyrate with a diabolical appetite that no man could restrain. Micky plunges and withdraws his prick in quick succession and with increasing vigour as it shafts the boy's throat and strains to impale it still further. Such is the force he uses that he risks cleaving his palate. Judging by the way the boy's mouth now grips his cock, Micky's victim will be feeling the first convulsions, convulsions that will culminate in a bestial final thrust and a suffocating shower of spunk, a drowning downpour of salt water, spattering, indiscriminately, mouth, face, hair. (And Johnny, joining them, standing overhead lashes the boy with a heavy chain!) At the same time, I allow my cock to stir and bulge and as it grows so do his eyes light up, flashing like a pinball machine. All the while, my cock grows. I grope it and as I talk dirty I move my thighs languidly; my arse quivers then tightens. He gives me a fugitive, sidelong glance, his eyes like a vanishing shooting star, but his desire won't allow him to equivocate. He unzips his jeans and pulls out a short but thick cock, thick as a clenched fist. Gingerly, he advances, rubbing it against the bulge in my jeans which I both flaunt *and* tease him with. I grab his jeans, undo them completely and pull them down. He knows exactly what's expected of him as he turns round, pulls his underpants down to his knees and waits to be fucked... What a surprise is in store for my stranger: for the first time in his life his arse will experience my plunging, sheathed electric cock!

I fasten it to my legs over my jeans and take aim as I gradually and gently start to enter him. Like a technician that knows his stuff I twist it, withdraw it, plunge it in again and, with increasing pressure, thrust it inside until it's pressed to the hilt. Then, while leaning with my full weight on his back, I unfasten it from me and forcefully grip his chest.

With the other hand I set to work activating it, controlling its power and intermittently switching it on so that his arse feels shock after shock sear through him with ever-increasing impact. I take aim with my crotch and thrust it against his arse. My thighs push forward and as I do so I discharge a greater and greater current. I can sense my victim's, or should say my guinea pig's body, meanwhile, shiver all over with pleasure. Every time I intensify the electric current, he moans with satisfaction and then cries out ambivalently. His arse reaches out greedily, spreading like an opening bud, finally dissolving, slackening in its powerless submission to desire. Suddenly jerkings and the beginnings of pain. As he starts to panic he tries to bite my legs, but is held back pathetically by his involuntary convulsions. Unrelenting, I double the electric input, jumping to 80, 90 volts. He screams and howls with pain and attempts to break free. But I've got him firmly under my control. 100 volts, 110 volts. I know the limits of human endurance only too well to realise that his pulse rate is abnormally high, that very soon I will have completed my task. Feeling him come over dizzy, delirious I realise I must act fast. At 120 volts, the nerve centres in his brain are being attacked. His brain is fighting back. He bucks and tries to escape. But I tell myself I must take full advantage of this sport – of my victim's pleasure stretched to the limits of consciousness; I must relish this historic moment.

My lucky victim is like Frankenstein revisited; this time Frankenstein The Erotic experiencing, through death, the philosophic transgression of life! Thus has *glamour* returned with a vengeance, all thanks to *technology*.

> "Don't be afraid of me going too far:
> you can safely assume that reason
> prevents me from doing so. But since
> you are tempted to disturb reason, I
> know you will not want to restore
> total order. All I ask of you, then, is to
> leave me to enjoy the agony of my
> wounds now I have learned how to
> find pleasure in pain."
> de Sade, *Correspondence*

I looked so like the photo-fit of the Grao strangler that was in this morning's paper that I panicked and thought of handing myself over to the police.

How our double-life plagues us! How can any of us put up with the knowledge of our true identity and not want to change it, even destroy it!

I was shocked to read about the series of murders committed by the strangler and about the hapless transvestites who are attacked as they walk the streets at night. We suffer from insecurity quite enough as it is, without being made the victim of others' fantasies into the bargain.

Our night clubs are so frightened of going out of business that they've submitted as much evidence to the local magistrates as they've been able to lay their hands on.

To strangle is an ancient, some would say divine practice. But who would think that a summer like this would produce such a concentration of transvestite victims and that the social repercussions would be so far-reaching...

Our precarious culture is characterised by fragmentation. Yet, like the mediocrity of our country it remains just this side of total dissipation, of collapse because and not in spite of the fact that it thrives on defeatism. It is this very mediocrity that depresses me, makes me feel misanthropic, murderous and consequently self-destructive and suicidal.

It was pitch-dark that night. The din of the exhaust pipes of our powerful motorbikes shook the foundations of alleyways and streets alike. As the four bikes rounded bends, like crazy missiles, their tyres screeched.

At the front was a red and black Kawasaki, dazzlingly chrome-plated, strident. It skidded and leaned recklessly to one side at every bend. On it Lo Rat-Penat led the way dexterously, intrepid as a cowboy in the deserts of Colorado.

We soon arrived at our destination – a dark street lit solely by a broken, yellow neon sign on which the word *Sarah's* could only just be made out. Only a black door with a gilt surround now separated us from the bar.

First we parked our bikes. With the eagerness of neophytes, Micky and Johnny, both Southern lads, got off their bikes. Complementary as the contrasting angles of a scalene triangle, one was tall, the other squat – although it was never clear who was who. Anyway one was short, the other tall and gangling like a bell's chiming stick. He was dressed in Lois denims, a waisted jacket and black boots of tooled leather. Wearing a belt with a military buckle, his shirt was undone to the navel, revealing ostentatiously, two firm, strong, worked-out pecs. The same bloke's eyes were narrowed, his expression sultry, impertinent, his mouth chewing on gum, the collar of his jacket turned up, his hands in his pockets, his legs apart and tapering down to where his sturdy boots stood. Above all his eyes radiated lust.

Crossing both their groins and visible through their jeans their cocks provocatively and conspicuously showed off their contours. Johnny's (I'll call him Johnny anyway for the sake of argument!) was short and dense as a fist. Micky's, by contrast, was slender and elongated as an effusive exclamation mark. Whenever his balls moved they would define themselves clearly on the opposite side of where his cock hung. If his cock hung to the left, a gorgeous, tempting bulge would come into view on the right. His forbidden fruit, his balls thus animated, had a life of their own.

Restless and randy as bulls, they stared at Lo Rat-Penat, Félix Trempat and myself. Félix got off his bike casually, stood it on its rest and took off the blue and gold fringed crash helmet which he wore and which made him look so much like a galactic warrior. Attaching it to the handlebars, he took out a thick, short chain from his saddlebag. All the while, he stroked his cock. A mannerism which was now second nature, it suggested that erotic stimulation was too good to miss for one minute and which anyway was an activity that offered endless, creative possibilities for sexual gratification given the infinite and subtle scope for the manipulation of one's tool. The area of his jeans where you could see his hand at play revealed also a cock whose proportions were something else! His balls, however, were another matter. Divided symmetrically as they were by a tight trough of a zip, you could clearly see that they were small and separate entities – in fact so smooth of contour that you could be forgiven for thinking that his scrotum was made of satin! Félix's singular gift put everyone else in the shade. Everyone was madly attracted to him, mesmerised by his eyes which, black and Arabic, were as dark as jet. At the same time cold and serene, they nevertheless concealed a latent rage which now and then flashed forth lightning looks, garnet-red and indescribably beautiful.

But if anyone was to take the prize for transforming the most humdrum, futile and banal activities into an exalted art then it would have to be Lo Rat-Penat. Born in Paterna, and ex-captain of the now-vanished Al Capone gang, he was today an indispensable member of the urban guerilla movement.

Together we had accomplished countless operations. All had been meticulously planned, faultlessly executed, successfully undertaken and with an impunity deserving of any military medal. His body, carved with the anatomical precision of a Michelangelo sculpture, was stupendous, athletic, lithe, agile. His face radiated arrogance, forbidding disdain: originally a cultivated expression, it had, by now, become established, authentic.

First to walk into the bar were Lo Rat-Penat and myself. A crowd of queens could be heard chattering like frenzied, caged sparrows. As they drank so did they shed their plumage. But it was the lyrics and rhythms of the bar's *romantic* music which had the most uninhibiting effect on them. "Life is neither heaven nor hell", the song went... "But my candour, my youth drew you to me... made our spirits soar... and when the sun began to set how vulnerable you seemed... You, you are the source of everything... my laughter, my tears, my night, my day... Spellbound, I live for your indifference, your praise. Life is neither heaven nor hell..." (And so on and so forth went the song, with its cloying stench.)

Micky and Johnny followed us in. Félix glanced around, his expression indifferent and, strutting as he walked, made his way to the bar. Total silence fell as the crowd realised we'd arrived. Only the faltering gasps of shock and fear could be heard – save for the sound of a dropped glass! Surreptitiously, Johnny and Micky signalled to each other, barred the way to the door and bolted it. They stood in front of it, their arms spread apart slightly from their bodies, their expressions abstracted. Then, as if the place had been struck by lightning, or invaded by fireworks shooting indiscriminately in all directions, the queens, cornered in a cul-de-sac of death, began to scream and run about in blind panic.

Meanwhile, we caught them one by one, threw them to the ground and stripped them of their jeans. Struggling in their underpants and acrylic vests, they looked like newspaper advertisements for incontinence pants and orthopaedic corsets. (Only Rocío Jurado maintained some composure as she crooned, "You are the ocean, I am your liner...") While Micky carried a small but pugnacious queen over his shoulder, Félix, standing in the middle of the bar, surrounded by scenes of abduction and rape, looked on impassively. Contentedly, he stroked his cock, as if frottage were a full-time occupation: by now it began to swell to donkey proportions. Undoing his flies, he pulled out his red, swollen cock clamped at the base with a cockring. The sight of a cock of such impossible, undreamed of proportions and thick as a black pudding, begged the question of how it would satisfy itself. But satisfy itself it did as he chose his victim, willy nilly, plucking him from the chaos of panicking queens, pinning him down as quickly as he tried to escape, forcing him to bend at the waist and entering him without ceremony, for a summary and phlegmatic fuck. Despite Félix's size, his victim's arse, sphincter splayed, miraculously accommodated the invading member and, judging by the ensuing din, suffered untold damage. Had his muscle, the elastic of his sphincter perished? Had the fibre snapped?

Considerations of injury apart, in and out went Félix's cock as senselessly, heedlessly he built up to orgasm. If muscles were sprained, muscles broken, the gut injured, insides turned out, what did he care? The only thing that mattered to Félix was to have a good 'fuck!'. His desire was an ancient one, a synaesthesic mix of exotic, savage sensations, noises, murmurs, violent caresses, smarting pains, lashes on a bare arse, caresses abrasive as wire wool, acts of penetration where at first the feeling was of velvet, soft and yielding, then of a hardening, a gripping, finally of a slackening, of a victim receiving eager to explore hidden, unfathomable pleasures.

Sarah's was wild, a hellhole... everywhere screams, howls and bloodshed. Blood ran off flashing knives every time Félix, his actions amoral, his thoughts remote, carved heedlessly.

Our victims' pleas were audible: Our Lady of the Helpless, have mercy! Our Lady of Distressed Fuckees come to our aid!

But help came there none as we revelled in our anarchic cruelty, as I revelled in fucking my terrified, red-faced fifty year old. My cock was up him and his flesh wept with pleasure at my sadism, my *liberating* sadism.

I ordered him to get up, knowing that his suffering would soon end just when he was about to come – what relief in death! And as he lurched forward, dead, so did he shoot. The taste of blood from the wounds on his back, inflicted in the frenzied heat of the moment, mixed with my spit, his wounds deserving of pain, glad of penetration, desirous of suffering. But although his flesh was only just alive, just resisting, my cock would remain deep inside him. Neither blood nor screams nor excruciating suffering would deter me from enjoying myself. His suffering, mixed with pleasurable pain, the physical pain of nails ripping flesh, of jabbing wounds which caused him to cry, the exhaustion which the contradictory sensations of pain and pleasure thus provoked, caused me in turn to whisper in his ear, before he died: "How could you have been so passive, such a closet case? All your life you were happy to go along with oppression and tolerance. Why didn't you protest? Pathetic though you are, it's people like you who have allowed this oppression to exist.

As I said so, I knew that this humiliation inflicted on a closet queen would be made the more bitter for a few homo truths! As for Lo Rat-Penat's particular vice, it was to see his victims fucked wearing their briefs. Just as the sight of an athletic arse is a turn on to others, so was the sight of briefs his fantasy. (Nothing is more voluptuous than the body revelling in and overflowing with sexual fervour – no dictatorship has been able to suppress the pornography and attraction of an outstanding pair of bums!)

Lo Rat-Penat's fetish was such that he never completely undressed his partners, always asking instead that they pose for him. He'd grip on to them, his hands like a vice, bite them, lick their crotch through their underpants, lick them all over until this left a taste in his mouth of the musky sweat of armpits and crotch.

And he would always lick them, eat their crotches 'over' their briefs, his hands gripping, stroking their cocks as these strained to escape from their confines.

At first, his victims are never as afraid of him as they are of us. He was too interested, they thought, in giving them pleasure. They'd think he was not as brutal as us who'd have beaten the shit out of so many others. But they were mistaken. Once dazzled by him, once lulled into a false sense of security, he'd take out his cock with a false, disarming modesty and fuck them always with their briefs still on, pushing his prick into the material as if the briefs were a second skin, a second foreskin, pushing this *condom* inside their arses, stretching the brushed cotton of their briefs, all the while accelerating, gripping their bodies to him, transcending all pain thresholds. Thus did he make sex raw, conspicuous, evanescent, polemical, a bid against censorship.

Sarah's bar was unrecognisably red now, spattered from floor to ceiling with butchery and blood. Micky and Johnny had turned the place upside down in their subversive assault on the premises and the punters, in their subversive quest to counter self-repression, force their victims to rub their noses in what they would rather have hidden. Oh how we reduced those poor complicit collaborators to pulp and carnage. Turning to me, Micky said, his anarchy suddenly lyrical, "Eugenio, you can see now why the strong must destroy the weak if we are to attain celestial freedom."

Normality had at last returned to the bar. All was quiet and normal if you could say that normality had ever really existed in the first place, if you could say in fact, looking around at these walls, steeped in blood, that it could ever return. Blood was everywhere dulling as it dried or freshly dripping from tables and chairs or gushing from the many cocks butchered by our sexual gang warfare, blood on hands, faces, legs, jeans, gaudy, awesome like thousands of bloody tears shed by many weeping gashes. Life seemed to exist after death as blood seeped from massacred groins and ran and coagulated in the clefts of pole-axed arses, savaged backs. Lips, too, swelled posthumously from the stings of bites and blows.

We did up our jeans and our belts, put on our helmets, left the bar, got on our bikes and drove away. His engine revving, his face grinning, Johnny made the lapidary, sententious remark: "Today we acted like angels of death. So what's to stop us from doing the same tomorrow?"

And with that, he flew angelically into the distance, vanishing behind a thick trail of celestial exhaust fumes.

The rest of us bolted the door of the club and smartly made away, leaving behind us in silence the dark alleyway.

"You make a hallmark of failure!"

LETTER 14
A letter to homosexuals of the 21st century
Valencia, 29th September, 1975

This letter is addressed to you queens of a future generation. A voice from your past is here to haunt your future imprisonment. What, have you still done nothing to improve your predicament? Then it's time for a few home truths. The heavens, my heavens are widening mysteriously and yet below, on Earth, all I can see is a vast festering dungheap. But I want to speak to the wilderness, distilling in my message the many silenced cries muffled by our decaying century. I want to alert you to strange configurations which I predict for the future. These draw ever nearer yet are like voices that, as each day passes, lose their sense. A poisonous, fetid vapour, a reactionary vapour that still progresses, breathes over you, makes your society moribund and drags you down with it, making you complicit with your predicament, rendering you both executioners and victims. A *new* structure must emerge, however, to combat these contradictions, the contradictions of being both victim and collaborator for which there has seemed no hope of entente.

From on high, my new perspective reveals to me how we have held the banner of defeat, pandering to a social malaise, as if we *willed* unhappiness on ourselves. For unhappiness is what sets us apart, a responsibility we would rather shirk in our desire to live for the moment, to think only of immediate realities, of the here and now. No thought is given to the political legacy, of this situation, to its *mortgages* or *pensions*. When this malaise undermines the stability and fabric of society, there can only be a cynical, mutually gratifying pact between doctors and the diseases on which they depend, between the potential for escape and an escape which is curbed by a social intelligence which would have us know our place. Thus do you *actively* decide to turn your backs on enlightenment and so behave like kamikaze pilots in a spirit of decadent defeatism – if you're going that far you'd do as well to commit collective harakiri.

After so many years of defeat, isn't it time that you actually rose above them? Learned to use flowers as ammunition, as your molotov cocktails; to fill the city with the erotic and corrupting charge of your bodies; to insult the world and its propriety out of the desire to escape the slavery of your predicament – in short to fulfill the harmless need of allowing your bodies to unite.

Gay men of the future, will you still be forbidden to wear 'feminine' colours. Will you at least be free to walk brazenly and openly in the stifling streets of conformity, to voice with subversive ardour your political rights? As for your relationships, will they still be judged by norms, confined to the insidious criteria of the best-seller and its safe consensus?

And your sex life – will it still be a furtive affair, confined to cottaging, to seedy, clandestine meetings, to undercover, nocturnal activity?

If so, recognise your oppression and let rip – deafen the planet with your protests until the false 'projections' of dominant morals no longer hold water. Have we not had enough of cosy illusions? It's really time to reject these flimsy models. Send in the raging Horsemen Of The Apocalypse! In the past, silence may have been a form of rebellion but today it is simply an act of collusion. To maintain silence now is to agree to society's dismissal of us. Quite simply, if we lie low, we won't exist. Either we raise hell – and come to life – or keep silent and remain entombed.

LETTER 15
To Aurelio Santonja from Carlos Besada
Valencia, 1st November, 1975

I enclose these writings of Eugenio's, which I think would interest you. Their content and the charting of his progressive decline into insanity give us what's a pretty well complete picture of his state of mind. Also there's a lot you can read between the lines, namely early traces of manic and obsessive tendencies by which the advent of dementia is classically identified.

As you can see, Eugenio had a mind like a sieve, so it seems only logical to me that this was his tragic and absurd fate. Although you may think this far-fetched, I feel that his mixture of hyperactive behaviour and self-destructive hysteria is largely influenced by an over-exposure to contemporary books and theories. Eugenio's deluded identification with a fantasy world or his soft-headed adoption of revolutionary rhetoric, viz. Godard's ropiest films or even the worst examples of Italian porn – led him to sink into an irrevocable state of delirium.

Eugenio is still making no sense at the clinic. He spouts nonsense as if he were pronouncing some obscure testament which, indecipherable, will never go on record. No one will ever be able to understand him anymore. It's as if the wind changed when last he identified with one of his fantasies – and the role has stuck! What I'm not sure about is whether Eugenio retains a sense of humour throughout his delirious gabbling. I almost suspect there is a macabre intelligence at work – as if he were capable, in his dementia, of a degree of conscious irony.

Be it progressive delirium, macabre irony, quixotic identification with a romantic character out of fiction, a desire to transform banality into fantastic ritual, one thing is clear: he has been finally ensnared, as if the Greek hero/victim of an inexorable tragedy, by a state of pathetic paralysis. Eugenio's real tragedy is in being reduced to a static, shredded, bedridden tatter. Not only that, but also his incurable state and his moments of lucidity, his realisation of what his life has come to.

To be honest I prefer not to think about it. I am sorry to have to say this but don't you think Eugenio's condition is like a punishment, like a slap in the face for what has been an innocent but misfired desire to enjoy himself?

It's already getting colder by the day and the damp grips one like a clammy vice. Don't let what I've told you put you out too much: I'll keep you up to date should there be any developments. Well, Aurelio, that's all there is to say.

All my love from your close friend,
Carlos Besada

LETTER 16
To Aurelio Santonja from Carlos Besada
15th November, 1975

Hello, gorgeous!

Don't you think transexualism is the only democratic option open to us? You should see all of us now. Anarchy Gadé has cropped her hair *au garçon* and dyed it strawberry blonde. She wears a scarf on her head of the boldest colours and an abstract pattern in imitation of the most exotic Amazon butterfly. If the truth be known she looks more and more like Marujita Diaz. Her eyes are wild, painted, or rather glazed, like Manises china, her mouth, made up with the gaudiest shade of red, as if aflame.

Anarchy's fantasy of the month is to be Queen for a day, the Queen of Spanish TV. The truth is there's no reason she shouldn't have been but she just needed social approval to do so. Fascism – if I may utter so taboo a word – only allowed *women* the pleasure of frippery, of frills and frocks.

Thank God this discrimination is no longer with us today. In the same way, it is quite obvious that Fascism produced quite a variety of inconsistent aesthetic requirements, whose sexual ambiguity was never acknowledged by those who were part of the system. Yet we are lumbered with a heterosexual aesthetic which has the approval of an unchallenged longevity. Satisfaction with the vulgar and a cancerous complacency combine to produce a cosy affection for everything that frankly is naff.

Heterosexuality is in need of a face-lift just as we *deserve* one! We're tired of the same old drab images. Anarchy and Marujita may have got the ball rolling. But if we don't all join in we'll never get to change anything. So let's get out the silicon and get onto our plastic surgeons.

That's the way to reshape ourselves physically and ensure change – in the best interests of a life of flamboyant and erotic adventure – indeed, a life become vocational for its libertine striving.

Clearly, any attempt at controlling marginal sexual behaviour only drives it underground, renders it clandestine, twists it and warps it... Yet it also results in the creation of a language of struggle, a celebration of sex unfettered, of *pornography*.

Many would say: "Well, what are they making such a fuss about?" "What motivates them to make life difficult for themselves?" But how little do these people *know* of the vicissitudes of sexual desire, of its organic irregularities? How *mediocre* these rationalisations!

Such would be the retort of us queens in revolt. I repeat, and any newborn baby would tell you the same, transexualism is the only democratic option for the future...

Don't you just love topless American showgirls? They have silicon implants and don't they look just fab! If they can be given bums so successfully, surely we can have our cocks dealt with? If not why not? For fear of carcinogens? What paranoia! The price of indulgence will always be cancer in one form or another.

Bored, tired and fed up with an alienating, inauthentic eroticism, jaded by normalising strictures, we are leaving to one side or saving for a rainy day the fundamentally important need for revolution. A revolution which will sweep along with it politicians, emancipated heterosexuals, legalised homosexuals, liberated women, the low-ranking military and children.

If only the most revolutionary and visionary manifesto were to encompass, unlikely admittedly, the mixed bag of conventional respect for baptism, gender, race, creed, civil liberties and the right of every child, mature enough to reason and vote, the opportunity to choose his or her own sex, then progress would at last be in the offing.

Acrata Lys and Anarchy Gadé are already heading in the right direction, paving the way irreversibly for a future liberal ministry in which choice of sex would be on the agenda.

They wanted to be women and so they are. It's a joy to see their flamboyant presence on the streets and their haughty expressions in reply to the startled looks of passers-by. It was as if they were saying, "Don't tell *me* that this wasn't *your* earliest fantasy!"

I quite agree – go for it, girls!

Love,
Carlos Besada

LETTER 17
To Aurelio Santonja from Vicente Montsomni
Valencia, 20th November, 1975

Dear Aurelio,

I must tell you about a recurring dream which brings me out in a sweat and causes me to wake up trembling. Nothing has both pleased me and racked me with guilt in equal measures more than this 'nightmare'.

My problem was that I've always fantasised about the inaccessible – I suppose because in real life I could never find what I wanted. I wanted such a specific type of man, a man with such distinct characteristics that only in dreams could I attain my ideal.

But one Sunday, around noon, I went to Viveros Gardens and, while watching the young married couples passing by, taking their Sunday walk, smiling, happy in the pale winter sun, I saw him. I had finally stumbled upon the idol of my dreams.

Checklist: clean shaven, round cheeks glowing with after-shave, a slight paunch (in evidence despite a baggy sweater and a Prince of Wales check jacket). He betrayed an air, too, of fatherly contentment and duty done. His hips were so corpulent, his body so muscular that he looked as though he might have borne the child which, with paternal pride, he dragged behind him, his wife, meanwhile, in tow, her arm hooked under his.

All these attributes are part and parcel of a virility paradoxically emasculated by the refinements of social 'status': for he conforms "naturally" to a codified sexuality, carries with him the kudos of paternity, exudes an ostentatious confidence in his heterosexual success story, all these qualities indicating that well-rounded happiness as the reward for these achievements. Squaring perfectly with his social ethos its affinity with the morals of his class is therefore unreserved and easy.

Since that afternoon, this model of success has been the obscure object of my desire. Whenever I look him in the eye, his eyes tremble for a second – what, I ask myself, can he be afraid of? – and almost at once he regains his composure, his kindly, benevolent mask, not, I might say, without showing, in the process, a little disdain for my impudence. He raises his eyes, now nobly, his look lofty as if his was a higher plane of existence and finally settles into his private domain, I imagine of sleek chrome surfaces and subtle, civilised tones of beige sophistication.

And so I began to dream of him. But what of his wife? Standing in her fitted kitchen, with its pressure cooker, its stainless steel dishwasher, its blender, its units of white formica, its immaculate worktop covered with utensils, still boasting their posh labels from Corty's department stores, all these indicating, of course, that hygiene is at a premium, I visualise her preparing dinner, a brand new cook book strategically opened before her.

Meanwhile, I'm in the middle of the dining room, looking at the little boy in his playpen and at Daddy, in the foreground, sprawled in a high-backed and voluminous armchair, upholstered in a dark, 'masculine' fabric, reading a copy of *Levante*, the colour TV in the background, and just audible, the sound of the news.

As he glances indolently through the paper, gleaning what he chooses to with a glance so cursory that he can only be skimming the surface, my every pore begins to respond. I become so turned on that I can feel a faintness, a debilitating vertigo, coming on.

A voice shakes me out of my trance: "Lay the table will you darling?" she asks him as if her very request were a flirtation, a form of sexual foreplay even.

He gets up from his chair and his arse moves with the alacrity of a swarm of worker bees summoned by their queen! His huge hands are shapely, as if chiselled out of Renaissance marble, yet at the same time clumsy as they arrange knives and forks... As I look on I have an attack of the butterflies, the pit of my stomach trembling, my heart pounding, as I realise that my dream is materialising.

I see him bending over the table and, forgetting his domestic task, he takes off his shirt and jumper, exposing his soft white back and then splitting at the base as it becomes a darkening, fleshy backside. Unleashed, pneumatic his stomach quivers and reveals a distribution of spare tyres concentrically arranged, ascending like the plateaus and peaks of a mountain range.

I come up behind him, attack from the rear like a vengeful shadow, until our two bodies are one, languidly one and mutually captive – complementary and united as two neighbouring cogs fulfilling, with synchronised precision, the same mechanical function.

Impulsively, as if in defence he grabs a fork, clings to it, without daring to let it drop back onto the table. But he stays put, without turning round.

He allows himself to become carried away. His heart is only too obviously pounding excitedly: it's as if he's losing control. Taking his hand to it, he presses it against it as if to try to regulate its pace.

His arse *boils* with anticipation and he positions himself ready for my abuse, for the deflowering of his virgin territory, an experience which he owes to my abduction.

The TV cowers and blushes and tries to whitewash the scenario with a collection of silly advertisements – lest its cathode ray spontaneously explode. The ditties of Persil, Ariel, Omo whitewash what they witness as they announce the benefits of restoring wool to its virginal whiteness. But a sea of magic brands has all kinds of erotic connotations: an encounter with my dream on the beach, flesh splashed by the waves and breaking foam, a fantasy of detergent cum froth. A cluster of black hair, fine as the lace on a wedding dress, surrounds his firm nipples. At the first frenzied bite they relax. His stomach, cinched at the waist by a tobacco-coloured belt, relaxes voluptuously as I pound its flesh; so soft is it that when I press my finger onto it it leaves a dimple.

He doesn't hold back: we're dreaming and so he responds accordingly. His wife comes into the room holding a steaming bowl of soup. Shocked, she closes her eyes. She totters but the stoic tenets of her upbringing ensure she maintains her self-control. She remains silent but finally bursts into tears quietly, her expression incredulous while she watches. Unperturbed, I undo his flies and bite through his briefs, devouring the glorious mound of which she was once the sole keeper. Poor girl! How easy it can be to see the security of a lifetime disappear before one's eyes in only a few seconds!

His trousers fall to the floor and a damp mark appears at the front of his briefs where my tongue goes to work again and again. My hands grip the shell of his rounded balls which, being so large, cannot be encompassed by my hand alone.

Joining his navel to the waistband of his briefs is a pathway of the blackest hairs which, as they descend, become thicker, signalling that a matted thicket of miraculous density will surround the landmark of his cock. Without stopping my sucking, I stroke and caress his firm thigh muscles, my massage working its way to his knees.

His cock then bursts out, a sudden sunrise, freeing itself of my mouth, stiffening to the point where all its folds are swiftly ironed out, his prick beating the air with its spring. Unceremoniously, his cock spurts into my mouth flooding my gums, as if my dream were telling me that time is up. But he won't be going yet, not until I have my way with his arse which at this very moment heaves and contracts in gentle convulsions as his orgasm comes to an close.

I take the initiative and, making him bend over with his back to me, his chest leaning on the table, I venture to trespass into his secret garden, two fingers exploring, the two palms of my hand pressing against his cheeks. The path is a dark one but my fingers proceed deftly, filling him, his arse closing round my fingers, closely as a glove, until his face begins to redden and dilate, as blood rises to the surface.

The rhythm of a motion combining hips and arse are electrical, technological, the work of an IBM computer programmer at ease with the insertion of a disk.

His wife, like a statue of petrified salt, looks on intensely, still clasping her tureen of *chilled* soup.

The little boy is now standing and bawls D-A-D-A, D-A-D-A, as if fully aware of the significance of what he has seen, as if precociously exposed to this (higher) sex education.

The TV still rebels, shrinking the projection of my fantasy to a screen measuring a mere 12 inches, stalls and finally explodes, destroying my dream until I find myself condemned to reality – in bed, on my own.

So, Aurelio, only through dreams will my fantasy come to life. Fulfilment through fantasy – through the ephemeral. Both of us know that love is only lived through dreams. But articulate it, translate it into reality and it comes to grief.

You're like me, Aurelio: exiled from love, always cautious about getting involved, we only know how to live by living a life of solitude, by conjuring dreams, dreams which dissipate as quickly as we wake up.

My TV has a computerised microfiche connected to it – and this stores all sorts of similar fantasies which I'll have to tell you about another time. Computerlove is the real thing, isn't it Aurelio? I dream of you, too, Aurelio, but do you dream of me?

Vicente Montsomni

LETTER 18
To Aurelio Santonja from Lita Vermilion
Valencia, 24th November, 1975

Dear Aurelio,

How are all you northern folk faring? Down here, things have
come to a pretty pass! The last few days have been something
else. Can you imagine? We all went on a demonstration. A *real*
demonstration and Washingtona was there, too. That's
democracy for you!

Life at the factory was in turmoil. The unions had called a
general strike and us two were the first to join it. "Lay down your
irons and yokes!" we cried enthusiastically. "Come on girls, let's
go on strike!"

We were so nervous about it, Aurelio: for the first time we
were taking part in a *happening* so to get ready for the demo we
spent all afternoon preening ourselves and perfecting our hairdos.
The leaflets told us to be at the Glorieta at eight – the irony of it!
We wore our camouflage patterned G-strings, the ones Loli
brought us back from America as presents, and our matching
platforms. We wore our summery, transparent tennis visors
through which you could see our fringes and Farrah flicks. On
our chests we sported the loudest stickers.

Dressed to kill, we made tracks to the Glorieta arm in arm. As
you can imagine *everyone* stared. A long procession of us screamed
hysterically but it wasn't long before a column of smoke rising
above Monte de Piedad and the savings bank made us scarper.
We turned and ran. The police were on us, firing rubber bullets
at us – Aurelio, they behaved *insufferably*. I kept saying to
Washingtona: "This is *war*... hold on to me and careful you don't

trip." The crowd went mad. Washingtona tripped over and fell, the crowd stampeding over her without my being able to do anything about it. A passing mob carried me up into the air, whipping me away from my friend – I was so frightened. In vain did I lash out and scream, "They're killing my friend you bastards. Can't you see the pigs are killing her?"

There was smoke everywhere and jeeps skirted the pavements, suddenly cutting through the crowds, hell bent on mowing us down as we blindly scattered in all directions.

The outcome? Washingtona was given up for lost. I cried with rage, finally reacting after my state of shock. Our illusions of going on the demo to find ourselves a boyfriend had been shattered. Instead we'd been near suffocated and treated like cattle by the brutal crowds. Mourning the disappearance of Washingtona I invoked Our Lady of the Helpless, praying that she had not been killed.

The crush had subsided, as the crowds began to thin out. Foolishly worried about the state of my clothes and my heels which were now hanging on hinges after the mad rush, I remained unaware that thirty or so police were heading like a hurricane in my direction, with every intention of making mincemeat of me, their expressions proof that they were not kindly disposed.

Forget the heels, Lita, for God's sake, I told myself. Run or they'll get you! Alas, I had only run four yards when I felt a rubber bullet hit me bang in the middle of my arse. I fell immediately to the ground. It was excruciating (in fact I still can't sit down). I struggled to get onto my feet, tripped on the pavement and found myself back where I'd started. On one side, I could see the police getting nearer and nearer, on the other the demonstrators hurling back smoke bombs. From my position – right in the middle of the crossroads! – stones and missiles of all descriptions whistled past my ears. I put my hands to my ears and said to myself: "You're a gonner – no Virgin can save you from this crisis!"

All around me, explosions, incendiary bombs, rubber bullets, stones, screams and there I was in the middle of all this! I was dead scared! At any moment I imagined myself pulped by the pigs' coshes! Then I felt a pair of hands pick me up and I heard myself praying desperately for Jesus to take mercy.

As I couldn't walk, they were having to drag me along the ground – as if I wasn't bruised enough already! I opened my eyes and saw above me a very tall young man, a bearded youth with long hair who was smiling at me. He was no infant Jesus, though, he was a grown Jesus Christ Superstar and beautiful with it. I felt as though I was going to faint any minute. But I must have been all right as the thought crossed my mind twice without anything happening. I grabbed onto his waist and we both glided through a doorway whose door miraculously opened, offering us sanctuary within. I threw my arms around his neck and wept.

He looked at me romantically and said to me in a beautiful Barcelona accent, "Don't cry my sweetest, the worst is over. Don't worry!" I stopped crying and gazed again and again into his eyes. He gazed back into mine. He smiled and I returned his smile. He kissed me gently on the lips and I swooned!

When I next opened my eyes the smoke that surrounded me made it almost impossible for me to breathe. The place was so thick with smoke that you couldn't see your hand if you stretched it out in front of you.

"What happened to the boy?" I shouted. And again, "What happened to him?" But alas it was only a dream! Or had he been arrested by the police? Yes, that's it, they must have arrested him. I thought I'd found a boyfriend and they'd arrested him, the bastards. My mind was in turmoil – thoughts of Washingtona, my boyfriend, my broken heels, my bruised bum, spun round my head. How many times had I heard my mother say, "You stick to the workplace and don't meddle in politics!" My poor, old mother; I wish I'd listened.

From across Mar Street I could hear someone shouting "Lita!" Was it my boyfriend? No, it was Washingtona!

"Darling, darling!" she shrieked. Laughter, sobs, kisses, embraces followed.

I waited shivering with cold, a mere open-weave shawl around my shoulders. Finally I saw him emerge, escorted to a police van which took him to prison.

I waved to him discreetly. He looked at me, his eyes swollen, his body stiff with cold. His eyes met mine momentarily, but he didn't recognise me. He staggered, clutching himself in the chilly, early morning air, sheltering the blows dealt him during his interrogation from the biting cold. Numbed, he was oblivious to the anonymous lover he had left behind him and whom he watched through the barriers of glass and the van's metal chassis, a cage not unlike that which would soon enclose him.

The boy was gone forever. Thanks to the pigs he was lost forever. But I can hear you asking me whether that's the end of the story or whether the Catalan youth really existed.

Well, I'll tell you what happened. Next day I found him in the police station. They let me give him a coat and a basket of food which I had brought with me. All night I kept him company. In my adoration I cared nothing for sleep.

Remember Marlene in *Morocco*? Do you remember how she followed those legionnaires everywhere in her unrequited love for that Gary Cooper lookalike! You *must* do. So did I long to be reunited with my boyfriend, my Catalan saviour, who had reminded me of what life *could be* like, of love, of being cared for. What a day! And all just for a kiss that came to nothing!

Here I am, my car parked in front of the police station. I'm so unhappy that words begin to fail me, so with that I must say goodbye, Aurelio darling.

Lita Vermilion

LETTER 19
To Aurelio Santonja from a stranger
(undated – FRAGMENT)

Matilde Belda has turned into some kind of Daphne du Maurier heroine. Indeed, she miraculously appears out of nowhere, where people least expect her, only to vanish as quickly into thin air. But I do have some definite news of her. She's left her post as teacher in Fontilles – not as a victim of tuberculosis as many of us suspected. No, she is about to embark on a life-enhancing expedition, take up her rucksack and join the hippie trail (in the queeny mode, of course!) – for a trip around the world.

I rather think, though, that Matilde let loose on the planet could be a public hazard?

(unsigned)

LETTER 20
To Aurelio Santonja from a stranger
Valencia, 2nd December, 1975

Aurelio,

No encounter is more tragic than the romantic kind. I can tell you
I had got myself into a right mess falling in love. My tacit links
with *normality* were destroyed.

As I transgressed the realms of decorum and tasted what is
taboo, I lived in fear that irrevocable damage would be done –
worse still, that my demise was imminent.

No, no encounter is more tragic than the romantic kind as
we know so well. If you remember, we were like paragraphs
alien to a text, yet intent on finding our place on the white page.
Now this page has turned alien to us, yellow, musty, dog-eared,
leaving only the sour taste of loneliness and a lump in our throats.
Is this how you feel, too? True, we put an end to a relationship
which presented all kinds of dangers. External threats out-
weighed its stability, indeed made it in the end unstable. I bought
a bottle of the perfume you used to use and doused everything
– sheets, pillows, mattresses, armchairs, carpets, slippers,
cupboards, drawers, suits, shirts, ties, handkerchieves, scarves,
vests, underpants, socks, books, shelves, suitcases, bags, all
the rooms, tables, chairs and fridge. Then I locked the door to
the house and hoped that you would be purged from my life
once and for all. But one thing you haven't deprived me of is the
right to rebel against the régime of my love for you. Our love
filled me with uncertainty and eventually augured instability.
Its legacy has been loneliness and apathy, a lack of respect for
an ordered life, for my barren plot of land, an unhappiness

which has caused me to live like a slob, to sink into a life of passive monotony.

Would we not have been taken over by vulgar, cannibalistic, mutual worship? Happiness for me must consist of stability: when I looked at you looking at me, I could feel myself losing grip on reality, my blood pressure dropping, my heart beat slowing down and my nerves beginning to prey on me until I was unable to hold my cigarette normally.

Ten days after Amsterdam it was all over. It's all clear as day. I can remember so lucidly what happened that there can be no possibility of deception. And if there was, it makes it easier to forget what happened between us.

I remember our room that looked out on the canals; your mysterious silence; our endless embraces. But that's enough of destructive and retrospective images. It's all over now, Aurelio, all over.

Believe me, the joy my seeing you gave me also disgusted me. How could I afford to lose my peace of mind when the public gaze frowned on our love which it considered to be so beyond the moral pale.

I remember those times when you were far away in exile and I carried on my routine life as insane moments, moments when the smell of the sea, a reminder of your absence, intoxicated me, made me crave my forbidden happiness.

My house, my friends, my contented, ordered environment, my manageable emotions – what price such matchless stability? Just feeling the contact of my feet on the ground – terra firma – however pedestrian you may think me, reassured me. For my vivid perception of things otherwise was that love could get out of control, wreak utter destruction, kick the crutches from under you.

Thank you, Aurelio, for everything you did not represent, for everything you failed to grant me. Meanwhile I – pathetic Sisyphus – remain in love with you. I know that represents the inaccessible, a foregone conclusion of dissatisfaction and failure but I remain, however, curiously privileged in my unhappiness as a lucid, knowing onlooker of my fate. Curiously I wallow in it while at the same time relying on the day it burns itself out.

My one desire is to see myself totally, cathartically consumed by it. By defeating me it will finally defeat itself: a love once furtive will die away, and we will at last be free.

How happy I shall be when I can exchage what was a superficial and inconsequential kiss for the most neutral oblivion: change will at last reverse change and ensure *normality*...

LETTER 21
To Aurelio Santonja from Momy Von
Valencia, 7th December, 1975

Aurelio,

Eugenio's much better. Lulú tells me so. She went to visit him in hospital the other day. He can't speak and he's lying down. At the moment he's all wired up, plugged in as if he were running off batteries. Lulú went for a wander, brought back with her a bunch of flowers and tells me that she met the most *beautiful* doctor. I can just imagine her, having "lost her way", having to ask for Eugenio's ward, a bunch of flowers in one hand, a box of chocolates in the other and smack! crashing into him, flowers and chocolates, Lulú and doctor, a pile of rubble on the floor. And Lulú, of course, having to be gathered together like a "helpless" Gloria Graham and rushed into the nearest operating theatre not without managing, of course, to cast a flirtatious look, slyly, at her knight in medical armour.

I don't even want to think about what happened in the operating theatre. Two bodies stretched out amid a sea of chloroform and medical instruments, their faces illuminated by the spotlight above. Their bodies, needless to say naked, in contrast to the theatre's hygienic glass and clinical green tiles. As for sound, pantings and breathless moans filling the morbid burial ground of illness and death. She tells me that she took the opportunity to try out a pair of "forceps", something which she has been longing to do.

While she was about it she asked for an analysis of her urine to be done so she could find out if she was pregnant. (But no such luck!) Somehow I don't think Lulú will ever have kids. Nature forbids it and, for all she might hope, she will have to give up on that one.

Women are so lucky. And to cap it all they want to 'legalise' abortion! What a waste! There we are hoping that we might become pregnant and find fulfilment through childbirth while they take it all for granted!

When Lulú finally returned to Eugenio's ward he was sweating like a pig. His hair was dishevelled, standing on end like a chicken's cock's-comb and Lulú's bouquet was in tatters after her hanky-panky with the doctor. After a while he took advantage of the relief nurse's arrival to bid his farewell.

Seriously, Eugenio is much better. We've been told that soon he will be convalescing and that, although he'll never be able to walk again, he will, if determined enough to do so, recover.

Best wishes from your friend,
Momy Von

LETTER 22
To Aurelio Santonja from Carlos Besada
Valencia, 20th December, 1975

Dear Aurelio,

This morning when I turned to the entertainment section of the
paper and saw that there would be a season of operas and
concerts at the Teatro Principal, I felt my heart jump and, for a
horrible moment, feared it would pop out of my mouth. If the
boy that I met at the Mozart recital liked classical music concerts
or operas, I might possibly be able to meet him again. "But will
he know what's going on? Does he live in Valencia?" I asked
myself. How am I going to bump into him in such a big crowd?
The first day they put on an opera I got there an hour early and
waited impatiently at the theatre's front entrance, hoping that I
might spot his face among the crowds as they arrived.

Just when I had lost all hope, I saw him appear, arm in
arm with a woman years his senior who I thought was probably
his mother. As he passed me, he looked at me provocatively,
winking at me to follow him. We went into the packed foyer and
as they made their way to the stalls I hung around nervously in
the passageway not knowing what to do. The boy's female
companion sat in the only remaining empty seat while he turned
and walked up the ramp. He caught up with me and as the lights
went out he nodded surreptitiously in my direction, signalling
that we should go up to the top gallery. He walked ahead, I
behind – just like the positions we'd kept to in our previous
meeting! As the conductor's baton began to move, earnest and
melodramatic, so did our adventure begin.

The top gallery was empty. I felt like I was the Phantom of the

Opera: soaking with sweat, I pursued him, galvanised by love and lust entwined. I followed him to the darkest spot he could find. He looked at me. I returned his glance. Smiling, he rested his golden head against my shoulder and, as he closed his emerald eyes that glowed like green glass, the opera started.

Once again, we found ourselves together, surrounded by waves of music. Smooth as the touch of velvet, our knees brushed against each other and I felt his hand move up my leg until it touched my groin. He played with my flies, bringing the palm of his hand to rest on my crotch, allowing his warmth to penetrate my trousers. Quietly I asked him his name but he wouldn't let on. Instead his lips touched mine as if to silence me.

They pressed against mine and his tongue invaded my mouth. Like a hungry leech, I sucked back. He flinched with pain and bit my ear. Excited we stared at each other in the dark. It was then that he whispered his name to me. "People call me Angel Doñat," he said and he hugged me, held me tight, huddled up to me amorously. He undid my flies and in went his hand. He stroked my cock through my underpants and kneaded it until my briefs could no longer contain it. Then his head ducked and he took my cock in his mouth, sucking it, drawing back its foreskin, either flooding it with saliva or drying it with such deep, gargantuan lunges of his mouth that I panted ecstatically, my mouth wide open as if suffocating from this indescribable pleasure.

He mauled at me so passionately that I finally let out a cry so loud that it filled the theatre with its thunder. The violinists stared at each other, astonished. The conductor turned in mid action. On stage, Tristan bit his lip, clenched his fist with fury and someone at the front of the auditorium restored silence to the house with an ostentatious pressing of finger to mouth.

Angel stayed put. It took only one or two more strokes of his mouth round my cock and I could resist no longer: shoving my hands down his trousers and grabbing his arse I shot my spunk down his throat which he swallowed, wasting not one drop as he drank. He got up, smiled at me and, like a satisfied child, licked his lips. We kissed and as my tongue entered his mouth, I tasted my own cum.

Exhausted, I lay down on the gallery's bench while Angel, looking down, took down my trousers, climbed on top of me and, with one fell swoop, impaled me to the hilt. The tickling sensation of string instruments in the background enhanced our pleasure. Meanwhile, Tristan and Isolde were looking at each other as if one had caught the other cottaging, in flagrante delicto, and was considering going to a lawyer to arrange a divorce! Now Isolde was claiming custody of her furs or jewellery and so it was that no one heard us moan every time I felt him push his cock into me, pull it out and lunge again.

It felt as if he were reaching my stomach, probing the *pit* of my stomach as if raking bits out if it. It hurt like hell when he 'stirred' my arse, impaling me so far he could penetrate no further. All the while Angel bit my ear, ran his tongue up and down my back, spraying my neck with his spit. As he fucked he broke into talking dirty: "Can you feel it now, fucker, or shall I do it harder? Move your arse a bit, that's it! Does that feel good, then?"

But I couldn't join in, my breathing now spasmodic, breathless, my moans kept to a minimum so that no one could hear us. The death throes of Tristan and Isolde's tragic love echoed round the theatre. Isolde died. But at that moment our backs were turned to the workings of their fate, a fate that would separate them forever. I could feel him boring into me all the harder, then releasing from his hard-pressure hose his cream so thick and white I felt I was going to die of ecstasy. So enmeshed were we, so mutually bound in pleasure that we lost balance, fell off the bench and found ourselves dragging along, as we writhed, any other benches that crossed our path – we made so loud a racket that the orchestra suddenly came to a halt! Universal silence fell. Tristan turned and looked at the auditorium, muttered imprecations and, enraged, brandished his fist. The heartbroken Isolde opened her eyes and fainted.

The audience, aroused by the general rumpus, were now standing screaming and whistling with such fervour that we decided to get out. Still entwined, naked and 'connected', we extricated ourselves, pulled up our trousers, giggled as we struggled to regain our composure, went down the theatre stairs and with some relief found our way safely to the exit. Don't you think we should pride ourselves on how daring we were. Who else would do such a thing? No one, I can bet you! But as the saying goes, all the world's a stage...

Well, Aurelio, now I have Angel, what can anything else matter?

Yours,
Carlos Besada

Aurelio,

I've been dreaming these last few nights of my man, I mean the guy I told you about in my last letter. I've been observing him constantly since I first dreamt of him. I follow him like a ghost from the moment he gets home from work and stare at him in stupor, dwelling on the most microscopic of details of his day to day existence.

He's getting up from the sofa now and putting his newspaper on the sideboard. As he passes his child's playpen he pets him, and poking his head into the kitchen, he sniffs the air, saying, "I'm starving, darling." She, smiling, turns round and, as she chops her potatoes, says, "Patience, darling, dinner will be ready soon!"

He goes into the bathroom, shuts the door. I observe him through the keyhole: he looks in the mirror and makes faces at himself. He goes up to the toilet. "Dare I go in?" I ask myself. "What does it matter whether I watch him from inside or outside – I'm invisible, aren't I?" So in I go! He unties his belt, undoes his flies and lets down his trousers. His long shirt with its fine stripes half covers his broad white cotton briefs which, undisguisedly, reveal the contours of a cock hanging to the right. He pulls down his briefs in one swift movement. They slide down his thick, robust legs until they sit at a level with his trousers. He sits on the seat, picks up a magazine and looks at it half-heartedly, skimming through it as he strains to crap. I'm only a few inches away from him. Being able to watch him, without him knowing thrills me.

I *could* touch him, stroke his muscles, poke him in the navel but I decide not to. I'm amused by how innocent his little face is! His eyes suddenly focus on a page and they light up. I move closer to get a look at the photos. I can see a ménage a trois in which a man brandishes his huge tool as if he were about to implant it in the vagina of one of his partners. The other woman, meanwhile, her mouth unbelievably open and wide, rims the guy's arse. The woman, seen side on, has her eyes closed and with her pointed nails scratches the man's back leaving brilliant gashes. As his eyes alternate between looking at one photo, then the other, I can see him getting progressively turned on: his cock gradually rises between his legs until it stands parallel to the pages of the magazine. In the lower photo, the man has turned one of the women around and, kneeling, facing her back, his arms firmly gripping her muscular thighs, he eats her arse. She, her head rested on a pillow, her arched body forming a pyramid with her arse as the apex, willingly receives his rod. Consigned to a subsidiary role, the other lies underneath them, plays with her female partner's vagina. In the position she's in, she's at pains to do so. So instead she withdraws her tongue and plunges a dildo – a battery-operated one judging by its shape – into the guy's arse.

The magazine's pornographic scene and the effect it's having on the man reading it have so turned me on that I can barely restrain myself from intervening and from transforming the magazine's fiction into fact. Yet I hang onto my prick as it rears up, in an attempt to keep it under control.

But what really excites me is what his own is doing. The way it rises between his legs and grows before my very eyes and how, his adrenalin peaking, he begins to stroke it, first at the top, then along its length, his head thrown back, his throat crooning. The magazine shakes in his hands and he brings it up closer. He scrutinises it as if he were an actor trying to memorise his lines. His legs open and gradually his balls slip down into the water below!

He stops masturbating and grabs onto his balls, pulling them upwards, downwards, stroking them, yanking them downwards again with a violent jerk until his foreskin is forced away from the top of his cock. He stretches out his legs and his balls outside the toilet, leaning back against the cistern with only the edge of his

109

arse on the toilet seat. As he pulls back his foreskin, so do the muscles of his legs and arse contract, relaxing as he lifts it up again.

It looks as if he wants to put off coming. He doesn't want it to be all over with in a few seconds. He puts the magazine down and sits against the toilet bowl, his legs together, preventing him from freeing them. He strokes the magazine's glossy page as if he were feeling its bodies' flesh and skin in relief.

He grips the end of his cock with a tight, clenched fist and 'tugs'. He tries to open his legs further but they're anchored. He takes off a shoe and, removing a trouser leg, releases one foot. Now he can spread them at will and swings them open like a compass, his stomach contracting with pleasure.

He squeezes his cock with all his might and jerks it off impetuously. He relaxes his stomach, gives his muscles a breather and stops suddenly, his face reddened with exertion. Gradually he fondles his cock again, keeping his foreskin half-mast so it looks like a partially peeled banana, and closes a fist around it as if to dam up the spunk which would otherwise bring on ejaculation. I thought for a moment that he had come but he just managed to hold things in check. He relaxes. He takes off another shoe, strips off his trousers and leaves them to one side with his briefs. He lifts his legs into the air and tries to reach his cock with his mouth! He extends his tongue but it won't quite reach. All he needed was half an inch more and he'd have been able to do so. He bends his legs again, twice, three times, but gives up. He licks his finger and pushes it into his arse which, in this position, he can do quite easily.

Soon his finger can go no further. He jiggles it about, sinking it in, pulling it out. Then two fingers are moistened, pressed together tightly and pushed inside again, this time with some difficulty. Finally inserted, his face radiates pleasure. Simultaneously, he moves his fingers, works on his cock. He pants, stops, starts again, groans, masturbates fiercely. Then his cock goes momentarily limp. He squeezes his cock, withdraws his fingers. This time he tries three fingers, the three aligned like a bundle of logs, and sucking them extravagantly so that the spit drips off them he attempts to insert them. But he can only get them to go half way in, something which, try as he might, he only just achieves. He keeps thrusting but has to take them out, remoisten them, open his legs wider and, very gradually, ease them down the tight passage of his arse. At first jammed, he pushes harder until this time they go the whole way. He swivels his arse causing his hair to bristle with excitement.

After his latest manoeuvre his cock is even bigger. Its head shining, his foreskin taut as his hands descend, I can see a drop of juice emerge, spread itself over his cock's entire surface, lubricating it.

His face tightens, flushed red. He closes his eyes as the muscles of his arse contract. His legs stretch, a single line from thighs to tensed toes. Excitedly he massages his chest, panting as he breathes in and out. He pokes his fingers into his arse, deeper and deeper, physical limitations conflicting with his desire. As he strives, he reminds me of my own ambitions and how they are realised only in dreams!

He strokes his crotch, allowing his prick to jerk of its own accord, to spray those drops of pre-cum which so yearn to mature into orgasm. His heart beats with increasing power as if to burst from his chest. He opens his mouth, runs his tongue lightly over his mouth and breathes deeply, his diaphragm pumped of air. Suddenly his body doubles over and spasmodically he shoots mouthfuls of white cream which spray mouth, nose, closed eyes and a tongue quick to catch the elixir. He bites his salty lips, his whole body heaving, exhausted.

His stomach shakes fitfully.

He relaxes; his body sprawls across the floor. He takes a deep breath. Spunk spatters his face and he licks any that is on his hands. Gradually, his massive prick begins to shrink and withdraw like a snail into its shell until his vast fair-haired belly finally submerges it. He turns on the shower and stands under it. Little does he know that all this release of energy has provided me with entertainment – indeed was influenced by me! Because I shall be waiting for him tonight in my sleep and will be showing him how worthy is my love for him. Private desires of my dreams.

Best wishes from your friend,
Vicente Montsomni

To Aurelio Santonja from Eva Nozinmor
Valencia, 5th January, 1976

Aurelio – I'm a whore!

The other night I fell victim to prostitution. I sold my body and
feminine favours to an old, seedy, debauched lech for *money*! I'm
a fallen woman. Even in Amsterdam, I'm a woman whose
notoriety is comparable only to *Jovanka And The Others* and to
Diana Winter in *The Fraulein Of Berlin*. I can just see myself
wanting to get a new passport in the hope that I can wipe the slate
clean. But I'm sure the truth will be closer to the song that goes,
"I'm a woman of vice because I know how to love..."

I wander through the city's streets, acquiring the necessary
technique which will one day allow me to take them by storm.
But like Xátiva, I'm still a novice, an apprentice, being one of
those who think that one is always learning, that one's trade is
never learnt and so it is that I have some way to go before I can
say I'm a *professional*.

Be scholarly, was my advice to myself one night. Ironically,
the same night, the voice of a queen apprehended me quite
unceremoniously with the following request:

"Darling, make me your servant!" I was so taken aback that I
thought my heels were going to cave in on me: Aurelio, that man
was as disfigured and moth-eaten as an Egyptian sphinx.

Indignant, I replied, "You, my servant? What a nerve!" and
turned away in disgust.

The old man shut his gob, blushed and thought again. "I
know," he said, "at my age!...but I could return the
favour...compensate in some way...know what I mean?"

"You mean pay me a fee!"

"Yes!"

I muttered to myself incoherently, my thoughts aflutter: "Lali, Lali, darling, you're being asked to PROSTITUTE YOURSELF! You, a queen of good stock, a princess, a *Queen* I mean, Queen of Cataluña and Cerdeña. And my ancestors Juana the Mad, the Countesses of Alfalfa, Torrent de l'Horta, Xátiva, Gandia and Cullera. My estates: the public toilets of Mislata, Bernicalap, Benimamet, my relationship with the Marques of Vagina, Duke of Chocho etc, etc.

Never was a queen of my stature, indeed Queen of Cataluña, so mortally offended!

But nothing was to deter that leech who stood stockstill awaiting a coherent reply. I, meanwhile, was in a dilemma – secretly I was drawn to the idea. "Take to the gutter, be a prozzie! Sell yourself! Give yourself up to the cruel manhandling of some hunk. Be taken by force (of course, being self-respecting I would have to play at resisting!), earn myself the position of sweetheart, make my bread as a kept woman and learn the art of permanent seduction. I can see myself used, abused, tears pouring from my eyes as he tames me with his whip, chastises me, ripping my flesh to shreds, lacerating my back, leaving it hanging in bloody tatters, all the while making me feel proud of my wounds – proof of services well proffered – an object of macho derision, made to feel guilt at my abject love...

"How much will you pay?" I asked. "Come on make your mind up!" I ordered as if parodying the macho commands of the men I'd just been thinking about.

"A thousand, no more!" he replied. What a cheapskate, I thought.

Still, there was no turning back. I thought suddenly of Lulú Bon's repeated advice to me: "Make sure you always look your best."

That evening I was dressed, elegantly, simply in a frock like the one worn by Blanche Dubois in *A Streetcar Named Desire*, a dress festooned with flowers, my head crowned with a tortoiseshell diadem, my jewellery costume – if the truth be told scrap metal!

My romantic dreams of '50s-style prostitution à la St Germain des Prés had been shattered. Curtly, I assented and we got into his Seat.

But the old man couldn't get a hard-on. His prick was as shrivelled as a prune. My function as prostitute consisted in bobbing up and down on his tummy button and humping him like a dog mounting a bitch. What a night! I earned my 1,000 pesetas which he took out of a shabby, black plastic wallet and which he had folded in four as if they were the only precious possessions to his name.

At first I refused them but he insisted that coital dues were coital dues and that he wouldn't hear of it.

Goodbye, delusions of grandeur! Farewell, fair dreams deceived! Whatever happened to the fantasy I had of lying naked on a bed, bags under my eyes, my face a mess, a cigarette dangling from the corner of my mouth while he, taking from his crocodile wallet embossed with sparkling gold initials a wad of dollar notes, proceeds to scatter them over my naked body, the body of Eva del Tibidabo, high-class hooker.

I've put on some Billie Holliday – she more eloquently than anyone, will express this dream turned sour.

I'm yours for 1,000 pesetas!
Simply Eva!

"I think I'm going to die of cancer. I live tormented by the thought of it."

Doris Day

LETTER 25
To Aurelio Santonja from Carlos Besada
Valencia, 26th January, 1976

Just recently I saw a short article in the newspaper headed
SUSAN HAYWARD DEAD. I'm sure you know about it already
but I wouldn't be telling you this were it not for a strange
coincidence. The other day I was looking through an old film
magazine, Modern Screen, full of features on the film stars of
Hollywood's glorious and enigmatic past. In it I found a piece
entitled 'Beauty Fair '54' and I saw that there was a missing photo
– there were other studiedly flattering snaps of Betty Grable, Jean
Peters and Doris Day – and that the photo was of Susan Hayward,
which someone had obviously cut out. I've been carrying possibly the same picture in my wallet for months. Dear to me as my
birth certificate, it's started to fade and lose its charisma.

Finding out the news of her death in conjunction with
this incident has left me rather disconcerted. The incident
aroused a great many emotions which up until now had been
suppressed but which only needed such a catalyst to make them
surface.

I'm convinced now that our generation ought to accept once
and for all the validity of the horoscope. I for one am now fully
converted to astrology. Our lives have a logic beyond the
understanding of the furthest planets – each night our dreams
are influenced by the ascendancy of a particular star, just like in
the tragic technicolour melodramas of Douglas Sirk.

To think that those mystic, enigmatic pin-ups which we all
knew for their winning smiles have all aged now – stick upon
stick, mile upon mile of lipstick, deployed in the service of
glamour, lacklustre, too. Without us realising it, these stars have

116

gradually stalked the grave. But whereas they have posterity in their favour, we, alas, await a *real* death.

Fat, gone to seed, skin sewn back with morbid facelifts, decay finally takes its toll. Delusions of immortality dissolve with the onslaught of greying hair. It only takes cellulite and cancer, the legacy of private and professional stress, and glamour goes to the dogs. An adage of that golden era warns that glamour is fragile artifice: "Glamour," it says, "is made not born."

As they age, so, mimetically, have we. Like the prophetic Baby Jane, we all experience the same grisly demise. Hollywood, itself, foresaw that glamour like cancer, is not nature but nurture.

"Now that I see her decrepit and weak, I realise how much I loved her," so wrote J M Serrat in *The Guitar*.

Aurelio, these winter days are depressing. Incarcerated at home, alone, my apathy is setting in. This pathetic, provincial, narrow-minded, mediocre town offers no escape. Stories of soured love haunt every street. I'm sorry, Aurelio. I have to admit there are some days when I shouldn't write to you.

There's no need to write back. All I ask is that you remember me,

Carlos

LETTER 26
To Aurelio Santonja from Pipi Yaguer
Valencia, January 30th, 1976

My dear, beloved Aurelio,

It seems like centuries since I last wrote to you. I'm sorry. I've moved house: I grew to hate Castellón. Thanks to Lulú I managed to find myself a flat in the city and since then I've been living in Valencia. Things aren't going as I planned but I've made some progress. I'm working as a window dresser for one of the big department stores and I have the prettiest home in L'Albergina Street. But my love life – that's another story. I'm one of those types that hankers after Prince Charming but as far as I know they're all attached. My boyfriend in Castellón started seeing some ball of fluff and that's the last I heard of him! Apart from Lulú, I have very few friends. I go around town all day in circles like an animal on a treadmill. For some time I wasn't eating, I was so depressed. It seemed as if not a soul cared for me. Bitter tears flowed down my cheeks. I wandered aimlessly round the streets and squares – Mar Street, Majesty Square, Pau Avenue – up and down, dejectedly watching the passers-by. It was like being invisible – no-one so much as noticed me! Walking one day until I was retracing every route, I bumped into Fernando, a boy from my home town, on Mar Bridge. Seeing me in the state I was in he said:

"Dear me, a man of your age and you still don't know that the only place to relieve yourself is the public toilets!?"

"No, I didn't know."

"Are you stupid or something? Get yourself a platform ticket from North Station and stop wasting time."

"But I thought..."

"Stop wingeing, girl, and get cottaging. Look for the sign which says Gents and get in there!"

"But I prefer to pick up on the streets!"

"Don't be so old fashioned. This is a post-industrial age: be practical."

"So, you think the public toilets!"

Without fully knowing what I was doing, being the country lad that I am, a naive, upper-class bumpkin from Castellón, I made for the station pissoir. To think I caught the train at North Station so many times... and hadn't the faintest! But once there I didn't have the nerve.

"What if I go in? I can't, I'm much too scared. What if family see me and start talking. How embarrassing! My reputation..."

Finally, however, I took the plunge. My God, I thought, what a stink. In my refinement, my sensitivity, I shrank back: all I could see was a row of wizened old men. I ran out at full pelt, taking in breaths of clean air. It felt as if I'd just had my head stuck in a bucket of manure.

But I was still tempted and, having pulled myself together, I gave it a second go. My knees shook so much that one of my stockings fell round my trembling calf. Plucking up the courage, I crossed myself, mumbling, "In the name of the Father..." and resolutely stationed myself, self-conscious as a virgin, in front of one of those infernal urinals.

I looked up and found myself flanked by a row of cocks as ancient as the Egyptian ruins. Their owners, standing in a row, looked at each other and unceremoniously masturbated in time as if they were doing the can can. God I was nervous! I'm telling you, just to recall the events is an act of will. What was an aristocrat like myself doing in this den of iniquity? But what was going on fascinated me, I have to admit. To think how little advantage I'd taken of this permanent and free live show in which anyone was welcome to take part... it was bizarre to see what was in fact telepathic sex because what people were doing was putting the visual on a par with the tactile – just by looking we were getting the information, the pleasure that until now I had assigned only to the bedroom. Voyeurism, pure voyeurism. And how magnetic this fantasy, in which the most intimate undressing takes place in public!

119

Outside, the station's loudspeakers announced arrivals and departures while we, in our private world, continued, oblivious, almost mechanical. I think, anyway, that the appeal of sex is its mechanical, abstract quality – like the cold pleasure derived from a film on TV, which however much you try to disengage yourself, makes compelling viewing. As for myself I am as you know as cold and unfeeling as a pocket calculator. To my mind sex is no different – it's *technology*.

For me the past has been full of suffering, visits to psychiatrists and the enactment of endless psychodramas.

But I've discovered that watching television, for example, has the same therapeutic effect as seeing a shrink and costs much less. When I lived at my mother's there was a TV on every floor. Of course, the idea is that watching it provides the perfect escape from all your worries and neuroses. I can sit for hours in front of the TV, watching the same film (Dietrich ones are my favourite), losing myself, with just a bag of sweets to keep me company. I love watching those epic romantic films, those *amours fous* with their Hollywood sophistication and those Valentino movies with their predilection for Spanish kitsch.

Above all, these TV films are intimate: it's as if Greta or Sara were flirtatiously whispering right in one's ear, saying the kind of hyperbolic things one would never hear in real life. Role model and hero worshipper become one, interdependent.

But, anyway, to get to the point: I must have been pretending to pee and trying to persuade someone to leave this dump with me for a good half hour – to no avail. Somehow, I told myself, I didn't know the ropes; I had to suss out what to do. However much the idea frightened me, I realised that what people did was to have it off in the cubicles. Suggest somewhere else and people wouldn't want to know.

At that very moment in walked the cutest boy. He gave me a hard stare and went into a cubicle, leaving the door ajar. Looking round the door, he signalled to me to join him. But I just couldn't. Everyone was watching me and they'd have seen me get off with him. But the boy insisted: in the crack of light from the slightly open door, I could see him clasping his cock in his hand. He was enticing me in.

I just had to pluck up courage and go in, simple as that. So up

I went. But before taking the plunge, I backed out again, started to bite my nails, look about me, vascillate. Then suddenly I felt my hand grabbed by his, as he pulled me in. Once inside, I saw his eyes glisten like headlights. His hands bore down on my shoulders, prompting me to fall to my knees until my mouth brushed against his cock. I smelt the acrid, intoxicating smell of his cock push its way into my mouth. My head was dizzy with fear and pleasure, my mouth sucking him until, relaxing, I began to feel soothed, drugged, hypnotised.

I remember it all now like a flashback. When I saw his huge cock, I felt another self, an imagined womanhood come into being. Still fearful, I nevertheless longed to be possessed by a member so colossal, so *masculine*.

I was a queen who, although in the know, hadn't yet been fully broken into; my hymen was as yet unscathed. While I sucked, my arse melted, as, obsessed, I watched his throbbing member grow. I pulled down my trousers and, with an about turn, let him fill me; once he was inside, nothing would induce me to disengage myself. I felt his verminous prick burrow its way into me, lay me waste, blight me as if in search of pastures new.

We'd only been having it away for a few seconds, when suddenly, we heard a frightful din, the sound of dreadful pounding at our cubicle door – our bodies froze. "Open up in the name of the law!" Stockstill, we stood trembling, terrified. We separated, tried in vain to regain our composure when we heard the words, "Open up, we know you're in there. It's the police!" I went all faint and started throwing up. The boy pulled up his trousers, opened the door and professed innocence, saying that I was ill, that he was only trying to help... but to no avail. Kicking and screaming, he was led away.

Meanwhile, there I was, my face ashen as I vomited over the police and cried boundless tears of rage and fury, tears which, when I recall the incident, flood back.

I'd like to tell you what happened in the police station... But, as you can imagine, in the state I'm in, I just can't... While I'm writing to you, *A Nun's Story* is on TV. This at least is helping me to channel my nerves in another direction. I'll write to you another day when I'm feeling calmer.

Pipi Yaguer

LETTER 27
To Aurelio Santonja from Vicente Montsomni
Valencia, 8th February, 1976

Aurelio,

For days now I haven't left the house: I remain confined to my bed. You must think I'm going mad and you'd probably be right when I tell you that I literally haven't left the house for *days*. I can't stand the cold light of day, the people staring at me in the street. It terrifies me.

Up until now, my dream was doing well but gradually I've become more and more alienated from my married couple. Every time she saw me with her husband – hers? – she wanted to knife me. Both of us had been passionately involved, finding that, in spite of her, we were quite at home wherever it was we chose to make love and swear our eternal devotion to each other.

She, on the other hand, lurked everywhere. She has a keen ear and she could hear the slightest fragments of conversation, the most disjointed snippets. Speechless, she would stare at me in mute rebellion against her relegation to the role of impotent housewife, to companion of the passive comestibles in her deep freeze, to her confinement to the celibacy of the sofa-bed.

How I had grown to love my solicitous husband, a husband who plumbed the limits of satisfaction, who each night penetrated me where no man had gone before!

Countless times had I come 'home' to supper late to find them both sitting at the dining table, she her arms crossed, her face charged with animosity, he his face beaming.

Last night things came to a head. My female rival had at last

put flight to the politeness and decorum which, with her upbringing was so ingrained in her – and rebelled.

Of this, I knew nothing. Before anything happened I was quite
oblivious. As usual I was staring at him, dazzled by his eyes!

Suddenly she challenged me:

"The relationship between my husband and me is contractual.
We are bound by law. What's your safeguard, then?" There was
a terrible silence. A glass broke – who knows how? A shattering,
like the violent interruption of a sudden heart attack.

I would rather have woken up but I was trapped: my part in
the triangle was up for trial! Pathetically, I attempted to speak
out but could only mouth syllables that no one heard, more
precisely that no one *wanted* to hear.

But the battle had begun. On her feet, she towered while I, on
my chair, cowered. Her look was angry but self-assured, a look
which reminded me of the scene from *The Violet Girl* in which
Sarita, sitting in a fin-de-siècle restaurant, observing the goings-
on out of the corner of her eye, her face partially obscured by the
veil attached to the front of her straw hat, finds herself
unexpectedly introduced to Anita Mariscal, the Marchioness of
an extravagant Madrid beau monde, a woman nevertheless
uxorious, who, dressed from head to heel in yellow, wears the
colour of envy. Raf Vallone introduces her ("Anita, this is Lady
Soledad") and the bitch looking into the distance with masterly
indifference, replies: "I see no lady here..." With that she turns
around, shrugs her shoulders and disappears.

There I was – a slighted woman, reduced to biting my lips,
mutely, passively, reduced to tears, my cheeks smarting,
reddening, burning with hate.

The husband, our husband – the one we both shared – deaf to
my pleas, lowered his eyes sheepish, ashamed as he obediently,
wretchedly, gingerly remembered his supper of boiled rice.

It was then that rival and I both realised what it is that faggots
and women have in common – that is, that we are not self-
sufficient. Tragic as it may be, we yearn for submission, slavery,
the masterful domination of an unbridled male.

Forced into complicity, we looked at each other in silence. Our
eyes met with tears, we realised our common fate. Face to face,
we were as woman to woman.

Women and faggots are marked out by an emblem tattooed on society's shoulder, the ambiguous mark of the Fleur de Lys, symbol of the rootless, the displaced, the marginal.

Lying in our beds, wounded by unrequited love, our arses await ultimate violation.

At first, I didn't know what to do. I was only dreaming but to what extent was I in control of my dream? I was helpless! Riveted to my chair, I intimated doom in the form of a debilitating cancer, infecting my entire dream. But I held tight, refusing to lose control, to submit to this tyranny.

Stop! I had to shout 'Stop!' to break the spell. S-T-O-P! I thought, but the letters swam in my head, refusing to coalesce, to articulate themselves. The words dissolved, gave way to vertigo, surrendered instead of asserting themselves or of restoring calm by becoming reassuringly *concrete*. What was this word 'concrete' anyway? What indeed was reality?

Would I one day find myself caught at the crossroads of two contradictory realities – unable to discern one from the other? Was this perhaps the erotic limbo, the fertile no man's land I longed for? An escape perhaps from society's condescending attempts to grant us forgiveness: something which our pride would never allow, our solidarity never permit.

I have the feeling that life in Amsterdam is a nightmare for you. So, Aurelio, tell me about your happier dreams.

From your friend,
Vicente Montsomni

LETTER 28
To Aurelio Santonja from Carlos Besada
Valencia, 25th February, 1976

Aurelio,

Since you went into exile, I've seen how, in your letters, you've built up a picture of Spain which, although subject to some lapses of memory, remains sharp and stimulating overall. Your perspective is that of the exiled man. Detached, at a distance, you see things with clarity and objectivity, even though your ambivalence towards the country registers both love and hate.

In your ambivalence you are not always fair. Like the minstrel out of Teodor Llorente's *Renaissance*, you mischievously embroider the truth. But one thing's for sure. You have plumbed the Spanish predicament, its inability to hold on to its liberal traditions and to oppose concertedly all reactionary obstacles. In short we lack political cohesion. Solidarity, itself, is an embarrassment, a compromise to the ego. Self-centred suspicion is the legacy of centuries of invasions, whereby other empires managed to conquer and possess in a way that we never could. But these truths are harboured, jealously guarded until the confusion of myth and reality provides a refuge from doubt.

Thus have we taken for granted that the past is nebulous, the future intangible, something which an ancient song in the oral tradition perfectly encapsulates:

> "Come buy my hut, my darling,
> My wonderful hut by the sea.
> All it needs is a roof, my darling,
> Four walls, a hearth and a key."

No country that I know of is as prone both to idealise and denigrate itself as ours. How masochistic we are in our self-pity, how eagerly do we flaunt our complexes.

Vice is perceived as virtue, defeat as triumph, humiliation as self-esteem, such are our perverse methods of consolation, our stumbling-blocks to self-knowledge.

Valencia – city of oblivion!

"Last night I dreamt of my return to Manderley..." Yes, I'd like to end my letter how yours begun: "In my dream, I was standing in front of the park gates. But I couldn't get in as the gates were chained up and padlocked. In my dream, I called out to the warden but no one answered. I looked long and hard through the rusty bars and saw that the warden's hut was deserted..."

Aurelio, last night I, too, dreamt of Manderley. And the people in my dream behaved just like they do in reality.

All my love,
Carlos Besada

LETTER 29
To Aurelio Santonja from Vicente Montsomni
Valencia, 1st March, 1976

Aurelio, dearest, I'm dying of insomnia!

Until now I've been unable to write to you – let alone speak. In my catatonic state, I've lost my bearings: I spin round on my solitary axis like a perpetual spinning top. Please forgive my delay in writing – I just don't know whether I can cope any more... I can't dream, my imagination fails me. I've been to doctors, taken sleeping pills but nothing can make me sleep, nothing will cure me of my insomnia. It's the only thing I can think about. The thought of insomnia obsesses me day and night.

Awake all night, I toss and turn, cursing the bedclothes, a glass of water on my bedside table, at the ready, my sleeping pills lined up like counters. Useless, useless pills! Accursed, too, is the night I first dreamt of him, first fell in love with that image and of my fracas with that woman.

I only have to think about it and I can feel my head explode. My hands reach for my temples as I try to contain it. The last time I had him I remember gently undressing him, kissing his every fold of flesh. I undid his tie, letting it slip through my fingers.

I unfastened his shirt, each button punctuating my desire to reach for his hirsute body. Once I'd undressed him, I buried myself in the hairs of his chest, tickling his body with my kisses, reaching, too, for his lips. The same ritual repeated itself night after night, dream upon dream. What at first was a simple need, became addictive, religious, inexorable.

Every night, I fell victim to my obsession, to my phantom lover, to my traitorous mirage.

Yes, every morning I woke up feeling duped, betrayed. I would awake to the reality of his matrimony, of his bond with my rival. But that was a fact I should have come to terms with, for I knew that theirs was a relationship sanctioned by law.

No, I shouldn't have let it worry me but jealousy got the better of me, jealousy at the thought of what they would get up to in my absence. "Would he be with her?" The thought of it haunted me as did my fear that they might be plotting against me, conspiring, working in league. In short, my emotions were totally at his mercy.

Impulsively, I thought of killing him. But, quick to relent, I imagined him naked, I imagined the warmth of his body against me and his prick which I would happily suck till dawn. I remembered how his arse yearned for my cock, reverently, patiently, how he craved the security of feeling me anchored within him. There he was, flesh and blood. How could I possibly want to kill him? How, instead, could I make him see reason?

But the factory of my dreams was on strike. With production at an ebb, I was consumed with fear.

I felt as if a thick wall separated him from me. However many routes I tried the path was labyrinthine, always closed. And her: a fading image she was nevertheless always there, always overlapping another, her counterpart, him. The two formed, in unison, a double exposure which I refused to recognise. She, the perpetual cloud in my sky, she the usurper – the terrorist!

Aurelio, our motives are one – murder! That's what pains us: our desire to kill is repressed by our protective instincts.

There's no doubt who has the upper hand in this rivalry. Doubtless she will win. When I'm not there, she will recover her strength, reassert her influence, repossess him, restore her rights as mistress of the matrimonial chamber, reincarnate what for me is mere fantasy, an imaginary channel for my desires. Yet for all its fantastic unreality, I'm convinced that only I, as an active partner, can give him the satisfaction he needs.

In my delirium, my insomnia I wonder what he thinks. Is he thinking of me, of how I satisfied him? The TV is switched on, although it's long before the first programme goes on the air. Given to desperate hope, I long for its crackling, grainy surface to bring me the answer to my questions. If he enjoys being with me as much as I with him, does he, too, dream of me? Will he be able to reach me in my dreams, to separate himself from her? Can I rely on him to do so? Will he want to? Will he know how to? Will he be able to?

And so, in a daze, I sit for hours, confined to my bed, in front of the television, mesmerised by its throbbing blankness, its prison-like opacity.

Then I hear music, music on the TV: "I dream of your voice," it goes, "your voice locked inside me... What shall become of me if some evil befalls me... how shall I live without you, a boat without its helm, lost without you, adrift..." The song depresses me yet more and I wonder if he would want to dream of me as I now long to dream of him. At this very moment, as I write to you, I hope and pray that he can read me, as if the vacant TV set were both deposit and medium for the transmission of my thoughts. I fear, however, that my message is impotent.

Blindness is the worst possible fate that can befall the voyeur. So, too, is insomnia for the dreamer. Write to me, advise me.

Yours,
Vicente Montsomni

LETTER 30
To Aurelio Santonja from Loli-Cock
Valencia, 15th March, 1976

Aurelio,

The boy in question is Angel Doñat. Suffice it to say, I've fallen under his spell. I would never have guessed! There I was, a woman of high social standing and pedigree, exposed, my heart democratically bared. There was nothing I could do about it. My sweet tooth couldn't resist the sight of this sugared doll looking at me as if the world was empty save for me and him. Standing in front of each other our eyes bounced back and forth like ping-pong balls. The sight of his emerald eyes made me gasp for breath. As for his eyelids, they were as fine as organdie, and his arse, his arse, like Eden's apple. His blonde hair fell over his face like a young weeping willow, his mouth, a smile stretching from ear to ear, was impossible to forget.

Like a bird caught in lime, I stood, watched, immobile, my mouth agape. My hand reached for my throat constricted as it felt by desire, while my body generally felt as if it were falling away from me, melting like ice cream.

All of a sudden, he vanished behind two billboards, one advertising instant coffee, the other proclaiming the merits of Max Factor's 'Blue Eyes'.

Imagine my despair, Aurelio, my sense of loss! To lose a smile so evanescent is to risk losing one's mind, not to say languish in perpetuity.

The second time I saw him, he asked me for 300 pesetas so that he could take his girlfriend out to dance. Quite apart from the fact that I found this amusing and endearing, it set me ruminating about love.

I gave him the money which meant that, if he were back for more, our friendship had a future, however limited.

The third time, I was prepared to hand myself over body and soul but he was content to ask for 500 pesetas. Oh, well, you have to take inflation into account.

How can I put this, Aurelio. I get so much back for such little money that as far as I'm concerned I feel he's the one getting the raw end of the deal.

Young boys these days take as materialistic and economic a view of love as we do a romantic one. We, meanwhile, will always have our twee ideals!

Lots of love,
Loli-Cock

LETTER 31
To Aurelio Santonja from Eduardo Pajillera
Valencia, 20th March, 1976

Aurelio,

You should have been at the market today. The same scandal was on everyone's lips. Pepe, the greengrocer could talk of nothing else. In the minutest detail possible I heard a story which has left me thoroughly disturbed.

The market was astir with gossip what with Doña Nati's tearful address to Juan Bolás' mother, as she clutched her son's hand. "Don't play the innocent with me," she rebuked showing her shaken, red-faced son, "everyone in the market knows. Look at him, he's only thirteen and he'll never be the same again, thanks to your son...The pervert, the disgusting queer, everyone in the market says so." (Here she pointed at the offending stall of lettuces.) "Everyone's seen him going into homosexual bars at night...God only knows how many times he had his way with my son on those lettuce sacks."

On and on she went: "An innocent boy like him," her friends nodding like turkeys, their expressions serious as a Greek chorus, their white lace-edged aprons primly starched, jewellery jangling, hands sanctimoniously clasped to bosoms. Doña Concepción stood, flushed, mortified, as she gutted her fish, scales covering her knife, blood veining her hands. Outraged, she jumped to it, leaving the stall to her cousin. Warlike, she made for home, her expression acid as bitter lemon, her arms chalky white, her legs gathering speed like advancing cavalry. Up the stairs she went – and flung the door open. Juan was asleep. She ripped off his sheet and stared at him fair and square. Still not a squeak. Juan rubbed two bleary eyes: "Yes, Mother?" That was the last thing he said for there and then Doña Concepción grabbed him by the tail, as if she were picking up a fish, and cut it clean off. Juan's body naked, bloody, blood spurting – and Juan's single piercing scream rending the air, echoing round the courtyard, rattling windows, reverberating round his own, dark bedroom. Erect, formidable, Doña C muttered furiously to herself: "*That'll* make them talk about my son. Now they can say he's not a man... *I've cut it off!* Now they'll really talk..."

Doña C, Doña C are all mothers here like you?

Eduardo

LETTER 32
To Aurelio Santonja from The Adventuress of Macao
Valencia, 22nd March, 1976

Dear Aurelio,

The enigmatic and ever combative Matilde Belda is back from
her travels and has been telling me her plans. You might be
interested to know that she has been producing an illustrated
history of homosexuality, an account which will take us from
Biblical times to the present day. Imagine what patience as day
in day out she scours dusty archives and the infinite shelves of
public libraries. The task is *mammoth*. One of the funniest stories
she told me was about the first homosexual man to make his
appearance on earth. It ought to be included, she insisted, since
no history is without its mythological beginnings. Anyway, this
is how it goes. It is said that our friend, Virgo Prudens' mother
longed to have a son. But, try as she might, she never got
pregnant. One fine day, she was in her room praying, forlorn and
despairing, and having nearly given up hope, when a dove
alighted on her shoulder and her whole person was bathed in a
light bright and sharp as a laser. Naturally, she was astonished
and, trembling, she watched as the most beautiful angel came
down from Heaven. The angel, kneeling on a cloud of cotton
wool which just floated above the ground, addressed her thus:
    "Mary, the Lord is with you; He has sent me that you may
know that blessed are you among all women. Father, Son and
Holy Spirit have been moved by your prayers and the Lord,
through the agency of the Holy Spirit who now rests on your
shoulder, will make your wish come true. For you shall bear a
gay son."

Having said these words, the radiant light went out and the dove flew off into the air and the Lord's angel vanished into the sky, dropping as he went a soft, white feather which gently settled on the head of Virgo Prudens' mother. Presently she bore a son weighing three and a half kilos who, as the story goes, was born by a feather's touch. The baby none other than our friend, Virgo, herself.

Did you like the story? Stories like this, be they related in chapters or serialised on TV, are always touching, don't you think? The other theoretical and very polemical tract I read concerned the new role of women in society and the way in which they have usurped the relationship we have always had with heterosexual men.

According to Matilde, times are changing but the sibylline and revolutionary actions of women have passed unnoticed. Our society is now suffering at the hands of scheming women, who insiduously and little by little, have gone on the offensive. But all this feminist fuss, thinks Matilde, is a smoke screen for other motives. The situation as she sees it is that women are seeing their traditional charms undermined. Tiring of adopting an increasingly masculine persona, they would like to see the vindication of their rights temporarily shelved. Matilde feels that men and women are swapping roles, that what is happening in reality is not simply an adjustment but an inversion of those characteristics which until now were safely categorised as 'masculine' and 'feminine'. But the situation extends to gay men as well: the role women have rejected is now being filled by us in the same way that women are now beginning to occupy the territory which traditionally was reserved for queens.

Pioneering, metropolitan anthropologist that she is, Matilde claims to have put her finger on changes in social behaviour, changes which naive sociologists and anthropologists worldwide have failed to notice.

Having thought the matter through, I think that Matilde may have a point when you consider that since male heterosexuals have conceded nothing in our attempts to establish our freedom, we have, unbeknown to ourselves gradually come to usurp the status formerly occupied by women. Strictly speaking, we have usurped nothing, since this territory has been abandoned by women anyway. At the same time, heterosexuals have subconsciously absorbed certain homosexual characteristics without compromising their principally straight persona. Women, now 'homosexualised' – that is to say more androgynous – have been able to get away with it since society permits them to experiment aesthetically with the sexually ambiguous and androgynous. But where does that leave us queens? Will we have to carry on adopting the subsidiary role once assigned to women – in other words wear their cast-offs? If so, where do we stand? Are we to be excommunicated to a nameless limbo far from the men we love and the aphrodisiac, their Brut aftershave, we so crave?

We ought, ought we not, to band together and open society to a liberating polysexuality. If this seems too theoretical, the only answer would be to fight to the bitter end, dressed of course in Dior's paramilitary Vietnam Look. Either way it's difficult to see how there can be any light at the end of the tunnel.

At the end of Matilde's book there is a strange manifesto edited by, and I quote, "a collective of feminist queens without vagina or clitoris", which rages against womankind. This misogynist diatribe is bound to get up just a few women's backs!

It's only a rough draft for what she would like to see become a part of the National Constitution, but I think it outlines many of the reforms which we as a whole would like to see widely implemented. The accusation that women are sly trespassers (see above) and the belief that their function should be purely Biblical, is not one which Mati is alone in sharing.

The document is divided into two clearly defined sections:

1. *ON THE INTERRELATIONSHIP BETWEEN MAN, WOMAN AND FAGGOT (Obligations and Duties)*

a) Woman, by her very nature, should curb all sexual and erotic activities except those which, to the exclusion of all others, involve procreation.
b) The wholesale banning of the Pill and all forms of contraception which jeopardise pregnancy.
c) The lifting of all sexual restrictions imposed on husbands and, by extension, the mandatory exercising of promiscuity. Women

will have the right to them only on the understanding that their demands be for reproductive or domestic purposes.

d) The outlawing of castration or of any other 'unnatural disasters'.

e) Anita Bryant's birthday will be declared a national holiday.

f) Women will be considered criminals and treated accordingly should they at any time transgress the laws laid down by the collective and the Constitution.

g) Henceforward abortion is illegal as are any pseudo-liberties which in any way impede healthy womanhood.

h) Womanhood and motherhood are one. Women must therefore conform to this principle.

i) Women must, by definition, be fat, with the exception of sex objects.

j) Women are forbidden promiscuity, a condition reserved for faggots and certain women such as hairdressers, dress designers, manicurists and lavatory attendants. The latter must nevertheless have a certificate proving that they perform well and full approval from a faggot. Prostitutes will have the right to service the men when they like; but *never* on Sundays. Failure to respect this condition will incur decapitation.

k) It is forbidden, on pain of death, for women to mimic, copy, travesty and/or adopt the mannerisms or characteristics typical to faggots.

l) Man, by definition, must govern woman. The latter must respect her master as servant and vassal. As the saying goes, "Slave first, woman second."

m) Men must govern queens who shall be men's favourites. In return, queens must submit to their master's wishes when appropriate: they must never be their master's vassal for man and queen will be, first and foremost, friends given that they will, by rights, spend their leisure hours in bed embroidering and crocheting together.

n) Policemen will neither be policewomen nor faggots and must be a minimum of six feet, two inches tall.

2. ON THE RELATIONSHIP BETWEEN ACCURSED WOMAN-HOOD AND FOUL FAGGOTRY

a) Faggots will no longer be considered the lowest of the low on the basis that by definition they indulge with abandon in all forms of erotica. Their inconsequential status, in any case, prevents them from being actively downtrodden.

b) Women shall be forever cursed. The Bible says so through no fault of our own.

c) Faggots will be the true women of the race, a fact which, in any case, is ratified by history.

d) Women shall never be faggots (see section 1, clause f).

e) Faggots will be within their rights to insult and disdain women – except the aforementioned sex objects, since these are the faggot's natural companion.

f) Women will not be able to look down on queens under any circumstances. To do so will incur the worst possible punishment – their permanent segregation from men as well as an uninterrupted period of five years' in vitro fertilisation.

g) Sex objects will be able to take theatrical inspiration from the behaviour of their gay friends on condition that their emulation be grounded on aesthetic or artistic reasons – or for psychological reasons where, in special cases, to abstain from doing so would lead to insanity.

h) From a very early age, the schooling of girls and queens will be co-ed. Domestic sciences will be taught as an inalienable curriculum in a climate of equal opportunities free from discrimination on grounds of sex, race or creed.

i) Women will always bear two sons consecutively, the older one straight, the younger a queen.

j) At the age of 12, women will be separated from queens as their education will henceforward be dedicated to religious studies and instruction on motherhood.

k) Queens and female sex objects will be sent to lay boarding schools where they will be given specific instruction in coquettry as the groundwork for their social role in adult life.

IMPORTANT: Classes in hairdressing and posture will be compulsory.

Mati's document is then signed with customary panache: "Collective of Feminist Queens without Vagina or Clitoris." As you may know already Mati's collective is a splinter group of Conchita Piquer's organisation. Must leave you now, darling.

Love from the Adventuress

LETTER 33
To Aurelio Santonja from Pamela Typhoid
Valencia, 25th March, 1976

Dear Aurelio,

I'm totally absorbed, infatuated, obsessed with my sexual fate. Feeling totally miserable and pissed off – and as a result quite disorientated – I decided, in my depths of despair, to contact counsellor Doña Elena Sanchís in the hope that she might provide the solution to my problem.

I'm sick and tired of explaining it and of going into the traumatic details, so I'm sending you a photocopy of my letter to Doña Elena as an indication of my grief.

How stupid and self-pitying we queens are in our gradual realisation of the awful truth. Yes, we must face the facts: our destiny of a bachelor existence confined to the four lonely walls of a house without a husband to protect us.

How depressing: my only prop is my favourite radio station! Write to me, Aurelio, console me.

Yours evermore,
Pamela Typhoid

LETTER TO DONA ELENA SANCHIS FROM PAMELA TYPHOID

Dear Doña Elena Sanchís,

I'm a young bachelor over the age of thirty. In other words from now on life will begin to go downhill automatically.

I work in an office and am well respected by my boss and colleagues. Some time ago a certain friend at work and I used to socialise regularly. We would chat, have a few drinks and, at the end of the evening, each would go his separate way. Our friendship, however, became gradually more intense until the frequency with which we saw each other and our growing mutual attraction finally led to us making love together one evening after work.

I'm not sure whether it was fate or intimacy which brought us together, but from then on we were inseparable.

The relationship went on from there, in routine fashion: we'd leave the office, go back to my place (he was forced to do so since he was married), make passionate love – I ought to make it clear that in this respect he deprived me of nothing. Afterwards he'd go home to his wife and kids whom he adored. This was until the day he asked me to take some paperwork round to his home which he'd left behind at my place and without which he couldn't do whatever it was he needed to finish.

His wife, whom I met for the first time on that night, asked me so nicely and so hospitably to have dinner with them that I thought I couldn't refuse.

When we'd finished dinner, we went through to their living room where we had some brandies and a good time chatting about this and that. We drank a great deal and we were getting

141

on so well that the atmosphere became extraordinarily intimate. All social barriers went down and the warmth of their company was incredible.

We talked and talked until not a trace of formality remained. The chemistry between us was such that it felt as if a warm electric current united us, simultaneously sent shivers down our spines. Intoxicated by our intimacy, it seemed that the only logical step was to get undressed. Carried away by the honesty and generosity of our emotions, I confessed my love. His wife, equally generous, showed every sympathy.

Once naked, he began to kiss me passionately. I could have died of pleasure. He kissed me again and again. She, meanwhile, took part also and enjoyed those first moments when we were all having sex together, as if they meant more to her than any of other the times she had made love. We were just beginning to lose ourselves in our intense passion when, from the floor above, we heard one of the kids upstairs crying horribly.

The enchantment of our perfect ménage à trois was suddenly shattered as its mother went up to its bedroom while he, suddenly troubled, moved away from me. I felt like a schoolboy who'd got bad reports.

His wife's voice abruptly summoned him and we both decided it would be better if I left the house immediately.

The next day at the office he wouldn't even say hello to me. He wouldn't talk or even look at me. It was as if his indifference towards me were his punishment for last night's events.

On leaving the office, he scarpered in his car, without so much as the simplest explanation for his silence, without his affection, his fond look without so much as hearing one word from him or sharing an exchange in an any shape or form.

I feel as if I have been banished to a desert. After the oasis of so many pleasure my feelings are arid.

There was no point in asking him for reasons. I knew exactly who was responsible for his change of tune and it was her, his wife, my rival. After a night of agony, scarcely relieved by sleeping pills and glasses of whisky, I decided that the best thing to do, albeit the most frightening, was to have it out with her.

So at a time when I knew that he was at the office I called at their house. At first no one answered the door. I rang again and, just when I thought to my relief that she wasn't in either, the door opened and there was my rival.

"What do you want?" she asked.

"I want to talk to you."

"What about? Why?"

"About our man."

"You mean *my* man!"

"Well, he may be now but not before..."

"Forget before...the past is over with. The only thing that matters is *now*!"

"You must understand..."

"What is there to understand. He's *my* husband and that's final!"

"Yes, but..."

"Listen, young man, there's nothing more to discuss."

"You bitch," I replied, "you fucking bitch!"

"Just because I'm not going to give up my man!"

"But I love him, I love him!"

"Not as much as me. Now get lost!"

In floods of tears I left the house and am still crying to this day. Doña Elena Sanchís, what can I do? As it will be quite obvious to you, I loved him more than anyone is capable of loving anyone.

I didn't want to take away her man. I'd be quite happy to carry on as his bit on the side. If only I could be left to love him. I loved him as no man has loved before.

Apart from your advice on what I should do, could you also recommend a good eye cream. I have terrible bags under my eyes from the stress I've been going through.

Please write soon; I think I'm going mad!

Confidentially and affectionately yours,
Pamela Typhoid

LETTER 34
To Aurelio Santonja from Carlos Besada
Cullera, 1st April, 1976

Aurelio,

Now it's spring, Angel and I occasionally go for the weekend to
Cullera. It's lovely, the beaches are empty and the holiday homes
deserted and spectral.

We were bumbling along quite happily in my car on the way
to Cullera, when Angel suddenly piped up with:

"My father died yesterday. Sorry, I tell a lie, it was the day
before yesterday. He'd been in hospital for two weeks and then
suddenly we lost him forever..."

He didn't say a word for a mile or two. We turned off down
the road which leads to the lighthouse. A sea of orange trees in
a most vivid shade of green submerged us, interrupted only by
a border of flowering oleanders.

"How did you feel," I asked, "when you heard the news?"

"Nothing," he replied. "It was weird, I felt blank."

We'd left behind the apartment blocks and the silent, empty
beaches. Not a sound save for the car's engine. Angel's face, as he
sat behind me, was enigmatic. He was staring at the white lines
in the middle of the road. Yes, I thought, death *is* weird... it *does*
leave you feeling blank.

I put the radio on: it was playing the sweet lament of Ornella
Vanoni's bossa nova.

I put my arm around his shoulder and he curled up against me
like a cat. I could feel him shivering. I wanted to ask him so many
things, things I didn't know about him... but he was somehow
stiff, distant, impenetrable as stone. Suddenly it felt as if I didn't

know him, didn't know what he really wanted. Was he seeing someone else? Did he love me? But what did it matter – I was with him and that's all I cared about...

The strains of the bossa nova reflected my thoughts as we sat together in silence: "our intimate knowledge, its every detail, is of great importance... no forgetting it, we must cherish it, whoever else should come along..." Angel's eyes were closed: he seemed to have dozed off to the reassuring rhythm of the music and the soft rumble of the car's engine. "Memories, memories of you, always return: the intoxicating sound of our car brings back thoughts of you, instantly triggering, immediately figuring, the thoughts you have of me..."

I was thinking of my father, my father who was still alive and thinking how absurd this life/death knife-edge! The thought of it made me feel bad, somehow responsible, left me with a bilious taste, a bizarre and painful wave of guilt. "I know another is now whispering in your ear, whispering words of adoration..." Was he asleep? I touched the side of his face gently but he didn't move. I ran my fingers sensuously through his fair hair... "But I know that as long as we live I shall carry on remembering... time may change our feelings, dissolve our love but our memories, memories will always be there... Nor will we forget the smallest details. A love as strong as ours is not easily forgotten, and you, you, I'm sure, will remember me now and then. Nothing gained by *trying* to forget, no good *wallowing* in regret. For years and years and years the both of us will simultaneously exist..."

We got out of the car and climbed the pine-strewn streets of white houses, glowing buttermilk, other-worldly now in the brilliant sunset. Hundreds of geraniums hanging from balconies stretched overhead like a fantastic awning. Festooning the ancient streets of Cullera, they formed a vast, shaded cavern of interlacing flowers.

We found the house, shuttered, smelling musty. The furniture, spread with dustsheets, was ghostlike. A few golden leaves from the fig tree could be seen growing close by the window at the end of the dining room which looked out on to the corridor. Angel was still sleepy and, without giving thought to what needed to be done to the house, we went straight to my parents' huge bed.

145

I watched Angel as he slept. Night was falling, the candle beside me flickering, swaying in a melancholy, fitful rhythm.

As he lies beside me, naked, I can feel his every pore sleeping a deep sleep. I can see the broad contour of his breathing back rising and falling. As if uncannily in league with the erratic candle's flame, the serenity of his sleep nonetheless betrays unrest, anxiety, some desire obscure and insatiable. Watching him as he sleeps, I can never sleep myself. Something melancholy haunts me, a feeling of dispossession, perhaps. Like a Javanese shadow puppet, the dark silhouette of his body is projected on the wall above. With my fingers I pretend I'm cutting out his shape when all I'm doing is following the outline of his profile from his forehead down to his chin. Carrying on from the harmonious contours of his face, I find myself suddenly interrupted by the absurd hiccup of his Adam's apple before returning to the smoother planes of his chest. From there my hand sweeps with involuntary ease to the plateau of a slim stomach. But suddenly, arbitrarily, a draught puts out the candle and my projector blows a fuse. Suddenly I'm without my screen idol.

It may sound like a contradiction but it always depresses me to be with Angel. I always dread him leaving me and feel he's elusive. Life is so mercurial. If only I knew how to keep him permanently interested. If only I could read him, know his dreams, be clairvoyant to his most private thoughts and secrets.

Perhaps, Aurelio, he has no secrets. Perhaps he's still a boy in an adult world. Perhaps, even, we ought not to meddle. Too much analysis can be destructive.

About the film I was telling you of in my last letter – it's all starting to come together. We've got the money for it and next week we'll do the first takes. I think it'll be a success! I hope to have it finished for the San Sebastián Film Festival.

From Cullera with lots of love,
Carlos Besada

LETTER 35
To Aurelio Santonja from Lita Vermilion
Elche, 15th April, 1976

Dear Aurelio,

The sun has gone down and the atmosphere here is so oppressive that all of a sudden you feel a wave of melancholy grip you like a vice and your mind plays tricks on you.

Carmelina, my little Washingtona, is resting, but tosses and turns in her bed groaning, "Ouch, ow... *ow*, my tummy!" Of course, she's suffering the after effects of last night's fancy dress ball at the Stag's Hide club in which the effect she had was like Helen of Troy. To the strains of the record *Heidi*, she emerged from a rush basket, her movements agile, suggestive, alluring, full of joie de vivre. Her act was so ingenious, so sexually blatant that many of the more conservative queens present couldn't stand it. Rottermeier, for example, a law-abiding and public-spirited citizen (courtesy of Maria Castana's morality) spluttered, "What an obscene spectacle!" But nothing would restrain Washingtona who simply carried on defiantly. At the end of it all, Rottermeier, an arch Victorian, was mortified.

Tears fell from Momy Von's eyes. But quite what provoked her to cry was a mystery.

"Where's my compact, my eyeliner, my make-up's coming off!" And so it was: two black puddles of mascara were running down her cheeks and mingling with the dust of her face powder.

"Ouch, *ow*!" Carmelina yelled. "What a state I'm in. My head's spinning. My breath smells like a sewer, my mouth's all sticky. Give me some more orange juice will you, Ruby baby, I'm dying of thirst!"

147

Dazed and wedged into her bed, only her face visible from under a light summer eiderdown – the only one there is in spite of the fact that, as I've said, the weather was appalling. And there's a chilly easterly wind bringing the damp in from the sea.

After she'd drunk her orange and given me a couple of bedtime kisses, she fell fast asleep. As I watch her sleeping I can't help brooding about death. Very strange, I know, but I feel very solitary, almost wretched like the heroine out of one of those exquisite Victorian melodramas in which the decor's colour scheme is all sombre greens and browns. She, a suffering soul, goes from bad to worse until finally realising, in a fit of despair, that her sublime love is but a hopeless dream.

And what if my darling Washingtona were dead? My heart skipped a beat at the thought! What if she had been ill for months. I imagined some incurable, terminal disease, some hideous form of cancer? After months of pain, suffering and weeping at our ill fortune she might have given up hope, given up the struggle against death and passed away, leaving behind her only the most exquisite corpse and myself, now transformed into a glorious heroine.

But what would life be without its trials and tribulations? How could we be after all, if we did not experience pain?

Again I thought, she's dead! At the realisation, my mind would go back to when we used to cavort about in bed. "Fuck me harder, darling. Deeper, as only you know how! What pain I must go through. But I love it all the same. My arse is aching for it. Go on, fuck me! I love the way you do it, the way you lunge, the way you misfire!...What bliss!...This has got to be the best time ever, don't you think? Go on, fuck me, fuck me, deeper, keep thrusting..."

You know what I'm on about, don't you, Aurelio!

From now on, I'm not going to let a single man touch my baby. It's happened before that she's been screwed by businessmen who've treated her like a tart, more specifically her orifice like a money-box, like a charity's collection tin, every time they've given her a squirt.

"I'll give you a good screw, baby," I'd hear from the next door bedroom, followed by a squeal of delight from Washingtona. I, meanwhile, would be seething with fury. I felt like telling them:

148

"Go fuck yourselves with a Nina Ricci lipstick, for all I care. Just leave my baby alone...!"

On one occasion I'd had enough. "Get out of here, you prick," I said. "Leave Carmencita alone." The man beat it and has never been back since.

Now she's asleep and I watch over her like a guardian angel. Through the window I can see a row of black palm trees, their fronds silhouetted in the night like skeletons. My darling's phantom death has quite disturbed my peace of mind and the security of love. I'm a gay widow...

Yours,
Lita Vermilion

LETTER 36
Doña Sanchís' reply to Pamela Typhoid
Barcelona, 21st April, 1976

Dear friend.

I have read your letter very carefully and have the following things
to say: Firstly, I know of no ointment that would hide the bags
under your eyes nor cure your dreadful predicament. Apart from
Doña Elena Sanchis' famous cucumber cream, our own range of
cosmetics manufactures an infinite variety of natural products.
But we do not have one to suit your needs. My only suggestion
is that you scrub your eyes with sandpaper and Evian water and
that you go into hiding for the next twenty years.

Secondly, as regards counselling you and finding a solution to
your "problem", I have to say that our consultancy really isn't
the appropriate establishment. We may deal with emotional
problems and maladjustments, but ours is a *respectable*
organisation. However, open-minded and willing as I am to put
listeners' problems before all else, I can assure you that I am
sensitive to your needs, that I would not want to ignore them,
and that, this being the case, I have listed below in the briefest
terms possible, the only course of action open to you.

1. As I see it your problem is a psychological one and as such
I recommend that you visit a good local psychiatrist.

2. As a logical development of point 1, dear friend, you should
stop your destructive ways before you jeopardise the happiness
of the married couple in question. Like all couples, they have
their ups and downs but once they have overcome their
differences, their main priority ought to be to conserve their
happiness. Instead, you ought to find yourself a loving wife who

will wean you of your misdirected lust, persuade you of the error of your ways and settle you down to the responsibilities of a married life.

3. What do you hope to give this man that he doesn't already get from his wife, and hasn't got since God first saw them fit to wed. A child? A comfortable home? The satisfaction of knowing you fulfilled your maternal duties, as you sit in your old age, surrounded by your children who adore you and take care of you?

Think about it, my dear. For the love you feel is a mere illusion, the product of loneliness, the solitude which "people of your kind" always feel. Come now, God will never give your abnormal relationship His blessing, will he? And as for the rest of us mortals, who could possibly tolerate it?

So renounce your ways and in that renunciation you will learn the virtues of manhood, gentlemanliness, dignity, virtues which constitute our sovereignty as a race, virtues which walk tall among those foreign, corrupt influences that so threaten our national integrity.

Yours sincerely,
Elena Sanchís

LETTER 37
To Aurelio Santonja from Loli-Cock
Valencia, 24th April, 1976

Aurelio, my love, how are you?

Well, what news do I have for you? Nothing at all. There must be some silly little gossip I can tell you! Ah yes! You know Lita Vermilion and Washingtona, two friends who fancy themselves as models for cheap photolove magazines? Well they've gone on a trip to Barcelona to complete their training on tailoring and dressmaking. But I very much doubt they'll get past the Catalonian border. They'll be sent back for being considered shameful degenerates or quite simply for being Valencian. Working as a taxi driver, I make sure I take home enough money to make a respectable living and don't have to behave in the provincial way they do. Although I don't like to bitch, those two are naffer than Bette Davis' performance in *She-Wolf*.

The lavatory attendant at La Pecera tells me that the corridors of the Ministry of Finance are full of striking workers. Solidarity is such that shopfloor stewards have joined forces with all the queens there whose ideological views make them sympathisers of Soviet and Cuban Communism.

Although the strike has been forcibly quashed (there were some ugly scenes with tear gas), the stewards are under house arrest while the wretched rebels will be given a pep talk the first dawn they're back at work.

But no one will feel sorry for their defeat. As I see it, what the world has lost in compassion, it has gained in cosmetics!

I'm telling you all this so you can't tell me I don't keep you informed. I'm such an old-fashioned queen that I never read the papers. The only political news I get to hear about from my brother's sister-in-law. But gossip and slander, that's another thing altogether! I *live* off it and so I must be in touch with my origins. I mean our oral traditions. Long live the oral tradition!

The hottest, most interesting news I have otherwise is that Purita Pi, virtuous native of Alginet, goes romancing it, or should I say 'coquetting' it every Saturday. She goes on the sly to Valencia to meet her bearded, intense, intellectual lover in the Café San Tarsicio.

But I can't see this affair lasting a week longer. Public animosity and opposition, and general denunciation of their liaison both from trade unions and left-wing political organisations (who shall remain nameless) will doubtless sink it. But nothing will deter them. They are determined to go public and scandalise the moralists. Stopping short of nothing, their love will be on defiant exhibition in parks, in cinemas, in football stadiums... A natural target will, of course, be the statue of Generalissimo Franco on horseback, and the square named after him.

As they sit on the circular sofa of San Tarsicio, the two lovebirds form an impressive sculptural tableau. In fact they look very much like Narcissus and Ganymede, once the two of them have got to know each other and discovered their mutual attraction. While one of them looks like an acquiescent inflatable doll, the other with an expression both beatific and transfixed holds a flask of poppers in one hand. In his ecstasy, he looks as if he's hovering just a few centimetres above the sofa.

You should have seen the waiter's face – a gorgeous waiter I might add – when from a distance he spied Purita Pi, Alginet's paragon of virtue, wanking away. What blushes!

Trembling like a crazed food processor, and not wishing to disturb their scene of passion, he put down his tray with its cups of coffee on a table of glass and chrome and disappeared on tiptoe. As you can imagine, the people at Alginet's disco, The Powerhouse, talk of nothing else. Nanci Night and Faraona can't stop criticising them. But they're just jealous and their sour grapes only goes to prove how frustrated they are. Basically they are in dire need of a brain transplant and an operation to cure them of anal retention.

Oh, how I'd love to strangle Faraona! Nanci Night is normally

153

lucky but if her luck is thin on the ground she only has to hear about someone's success and she is consumed with jealousy. Her one ambition is to get married. As well it might be because she's not getting any younger and there's every chance that she'll end up on the shelf.

I for one don't bother with Alginet's disco or Sarah's for that matter. It's full of airheads that get on your tits quite apart from the fact that going there has become a health hazard: the other night some maniacs went there, wielding knives and chains, leaving the clientele half-dead with their private parts rearranged. Serves them right, if you ask me!

A new disco The Stag's Hide has just opened. It's so wonderful and the perfect place to smooch on the dance floor – everyone is there (the crème de la crème, I mean) and maximum effort is made to dress like the glitterati out of *Hello!* There's no better way of finding out what people will be wearing next year!

Well, darling, after having filled you in on all these events, I wish *you* an equally entertaining time!

Sweetheart... behave yourself and don't forget to write.

Loli-Cock

PS. I forgot to tell you that I'm also working in a factory which makes the cutest First Holy Communion and Confirmation dresses.

LETTER 28
To Aurelio Santonja from Lulú Bon
Valencia, 25th April, 1976

Life plods on here, darling, but for one incredible but true
scandal! Yesterday Lita Vermilion and Washingtona went to
Barcelona. Something to do with their 'work', I suppose, now
that they're working in dressmaking. You know what they're
like. They'll be seeing old friends, making new ones, squeezing
the last drop out of everything they do and coming home again
deeply satisfied that they'll have left behind them a trail of scandals
– incorrigible girls that they are! – and a wake of Northern,
Catalan types aghast and mortified at the obscenities they'll have
witnessed.

I can see the day coming when they're declared a public
hazard, a threat on a national scale: the river Ebro border to
Catalonia will be infested with crocodiles to stop us getting
across. I presume you got a postcard of Moreneta acting in the
Molino Theatre. The midget may be Catalan but, stood beside
our hunchbacked Virgin of the Lost Souls, she wouldn't so much
as reach the top of her shoes. The two of them, I'm sure, are intimate
friends, speak the same language and will no doubt be highly
respected for their gentleness and simple-mindedness when they
go to Heaven.

On the other hand, who knows, they might be expelled for
being poofters! Talking of virgins, I knew there was another
piece of gossip I had to tell you. Have I ever spoken to you about
these two friends, Acrata Lys and Anarchy Gadé that want to be
transexuals? Come to think about it, I think I may have done.
Well, anyway, as they need money to go to Casablanca for the
operation they had to find a way of getting lots of cash fast. So
they picked up this old codger in the Astoria Palace Hotel and

155

took him to Saler Park. They nicked loads of money, an extremely expensive ring and not only left him without a car but they undressed him, too. He had to make his way back to the hotel at dawn naked, covering his arse out of sheer embarrassment with a piece of newspaper. But the poor things were arrested yesterday and have been put in prison indefinitely. I enclose a press cutting which tells you all about it.

When I was told about it, I was so shocked that my mink fell to the floor and the blood rushed to my skin. I couldn't believe it, my two darlings in the jug! Don't you think it's such a waste – such beautiful creatures! They ought, at the very least, to be honoured with the Garter of Isabel the Catholic, like Lola Flores was, for their symbolic triumph over the macho pigs. After all, the wheeze was an unprecedented victory!

To begin at the beginning, Acrata Lys was stroking her undies, and unhitching her coffee coloured satin skirt in no uncertain terms – and with a dexterity admirably affected for someone of no experience. Looking at herself out of the corner of her eye in the reflection of the shop window in which there was a display of Soral bras, she thought to herself:

"Yes, very nice... a true woman, indeed!" Gleefully she licked her lips to bring out their gloss. The night's neon lights of the Rodrigo Botet Square shone on a confusion of cars and crowds of people going in and out of the bars and discos of the Palace Hotel. It must have seemed quite a party.

Anarchy Gadé, as if the winner in an erotic version of the Eurovision Song Contest, opened the door of a watermelon-red Ford Fiesta and called out to Acrata, her voice so shrill, theatrical and effeminate that it might well have given her sex away.

"Acrata, darling, hurry up! Stop scratching your crotch, sweetheart. Get a move on!"

Anarchy leant back in the front passenger seat and shut the door. Acrata Lys's hair is dyed a deep shade of carrot but its distinguishing feature is that it hangs straight as Garbo's in the last scene of *Queen Christina*. Her expression is indolent, her eyes vacant. Her figure is fantastic, a bit like a hula-hoop dancer whose multiple gyrations and anatomical permutations are suddenly fixed in one incredible lightning shutter still. Acrata obeyed, her act severely hindered, however, by her high heels

156

(courtesy of Grazielle Thrift Stores) and her hip-hugging micro mini.

"Anarchy, my skirt's killing me!"

"Hurry up... just make sure we can't see them... I mean it!"

Once Acrata was inside, the engine revved, a long, hungry, erotic rev until, suddenly, the car was out of sight.

The car had joined a queue going up Saler Street. Did you know that the developers have moved in on the area, are buying the land and planning to rebuild on it? The filthy conspirators are about to destroy the country's most thriving and romantic cruising-ground!

Driving up Saler Street, the atmosphere thickened with the sickly smell of overcrowding orange blossom – a smell which, at night never seems to pall. The radio cassette was probably playing, "Unfaithful wife if you and God decide to speak..."

"Darling, faster, faster, I love the speed... WOOOOH!"

"I love the wind blowing in my face. My hair – it's just like one of those Elnett hairspray ads."

A Spring full moon, round and pale as a pumpkin, was an ironic forecast of the night's events.

Acrata, looking perfectly doll-like, sat in the back seat, fiddling lazily with a depilator wrapped in yesterday's paper.

Very probably the car's driver took advantage of the various gear changes to stroke sweet Anarchy's knee. She, in turn, complied, flirtatious, playing to the rules of a game which obviously she had to pretend were second nature. Of course, at the back of her mind, was the thought of the money she would earn for her services – foreplay to the final kill!

These two girls, pretty as a picture in their organdie frocks, have been working in the world's oldest profession for only a year. But their long, dyed tresses, their dozen or so hormone injections, the frocks which they stole off their sister and their unambiguous coat of warpaint account for their status as the most coveted whores in town.

Of course, their clients must *know*. People aren't *that* stupid but, anyway, it doesn't matter. There's a certain glamour, it seems, in doing it with 'hybrids'. And to justify themselves they'd prob-ably have said, "I had no idea that those cocksuckers were..." as

157

a prelude to telling their colleagues at the office who were no doubt envious of their capacity for perversion and experimentation, all for a mere two thousand pesetas.

"You've got to see it to believe it!" and so on.

When they got to the park, they parked among the pines and the thick vegetation. In the distance there were other moonlit cars, their engines and lights switched off, all noise suspended in silence, their windows steamed up.

The man leant his seat back, turned round and grabbed Acrata, releasing her sexy, albeit synthetic tits.

Anarchy joined them and with slick professionalism, undid his flies. Deftly, speedily as a typist on 80 words a minute, her tits gripped round his cock, she began to wank him off at full pelt. But what he wanted was to screw her, not be masturbated. As you can imagine, the thing was to avoid this happening: their cocks were, of course, concealed, pulled back between their legs, stuck down with sticky plaster.

"Stop masturbating me. For two thousand pesetas I deserve a good screw."

"Darling, don't you see we're virgins. We're not even eighteen. Come on, you wouldn't want the police...Tell you what, we'll give you the best blow job you've ever had! Just you wait!"

"Don't piss about. If you want to wank do it yourselves."

"I'd love to, believe me, but I'm having my period and I can't take out my tampon, so..."

Acrata Lys stopped playing with him for a moment and lit up a cigarette. She inhaled voluptuously, blew out her smoke and got to work on him again in spite of his protests.

Movements inside the car were like those of an articulated lorry. Sandwiching him in the middle, they went through their entire repertoire (no doubt learned from a comprehensive manual, an A to Z of sexual perversions). Coming as if there were no tomorrow, their punter finally lay back in his seat lulled half-asleep with so much pleasure.

I think from then on, however, things began to nosedive. Of course, when it came to the trial everyone had a different story to tell! My darlings told the court that they had stolen nothing. As for *him*, he's a real bullshitter, they said. Their chances of being found innocent were slender – it looked from the start that they would be found guilty from the word go. But they stuck to their guns.

In one serious conversation we had, that's if they can be serious about anything else, they confided the truth, or as near to it as they could.

Their lawyer had tried to extract it from them, saying that he would perform better if he knew exactly what happened.

The story goes that because of the general commotion in the car, the door of the glove compartment fell open. Next to the road map and a pair of condoms there was a wallet. It was an opportunity too good to miss. Acrata grabbed hold of it and, seeing that it contained 25,000 pesetas, surreptitiously removed the notes and returned the wallet to the compartment.

She says that she'd simply 'borrowed' the money and that she intended to pay it back. At the time he discovered that Anarchy, meanwhile, had managed to steal his gold wedding ring while she'd been stroking his hand. When he realised this the man was transformed into a raging bull or a caveman drawn out of his cave by the challenging sounds of a predator.

Anarchy's story was that she'd been *given* the gold ring as a present but that now he couldn't remember having done so. Pleading innocence, she swore she'd never stolen anything in her life. A torrent of excuses: chaos reigned in the car, no one really knew what anyone was doing, their lovemaking knew no bounds, with the surrounding mist no one could be sure of what anyone was doing, gestures expressing confusion accompanying every excuse, designed of course to win the jury's sympathy.

But he would have nothing of this, roaring with anger, his face a darker shade of beetroot:

"You bloody queers...You stole my money, took my gold wedding ring. My wife nearly killed me when she saw it wasn't there." And so on and so forth.

Of course, they played dumb, referring not to the way in which he'd wised up in the car or how Acrata had aimed a toy gun at him, how Anarchy had whipped out her depilator, had thrashed him on the head with it, Acrata, meanwhile, screaming that she stop lest she kill him, but Anarchy pounding anyway until his whole face was covered in blood and his skull lacerated by four nails' worth of scars.

No doubt the next day no one would have recognised him. What wicked, callous creatures the both of them. To cap it all, they undressed him, made off with his car and left him to go to the hotel naked, his privates barely covered by a hand placed in front, another at the back in his vain attempts to hide his bum from the world at large.

Lots of love from your friend, your fellow sodomite,
Lulú Bon

P.S. When the trial finishes, I'll let you know the outcome. The lawyer says that the mildest sentence they can expect is six months in prison but that he will push his hardest for their acquittal.

PRESS CUTTING

The court found the two defendants guilty of theft by virtue of their having appropriated another man's property, for motives of aggrandisement. The theft was carried out without violence or harassment given that intimidation of their victim only came about upon his discovery of the theft by the two defendants of money and a ring and of his reaction to this discovery. In consideration of the two defendants' psychological stability, it was decided that their actions constituted cunning, deceit and deliberate intent to steal. In spite of their dubious sexuality, they were not granted diminished responsibility. In view of this the court pronounced X and Y guilty of theft holding them answerable to a fine of 35,000 pesetas with additional penalties of overnight custody subject to six months' imprisonment should either party fail to act in accordance with the law.

Valencia, 15th June, 1976

LETTER 39
To Aurelio Santonja from Lulú Bon
Valencia, 26th April, 1976

Dear Aurelio,

I hate to have to tell you this but Lita and Washingtona died yesterday in a car accident on their way to Barcelona. According to what I've heard they were in the vicinity of Sagunto when it happened. I'm still shellshocked by it all! I know how much you loved them.

The last two days have been exhausting. First there was the news which hit me out of the blue. Then there were the funeral arrangements. I went over to console one family, then to the other where I consoled mother number two. Then, of course, there were all the legal documents to deal with, discussions of what mass to have, the hiring of the hearse, payment thereof. All this was seen to without a break because as you can imagine I had to deal with everything. Neither Lita's mother (a native of Puig) nor Washingtona's were in a fit state of mind to make any arrangements themselves. Poor things. It just hasn't sunk in yet. Come to think about it, it hasn't with me either.

At half past six in the afternoon, I left the two mothers in the nearby station so that they could go home. On my way back I suddenly started crying buckets. As you can imagine I hadn't been able to do so until then there was so much to do. But I couldn't hold back any longer. I might not seem that type of person but, deep down, I'm as vulnerable a human being as anyone else.

It's nightime now. It's a horribly dark night and I'm haunted by their presence. I'd almost go as far as to say that their ghost is following me everywhere, plaguing me with a strange sense of guilt.

I'm going to take a couple of sleeping pills. I'll carry on my letter when I wake up...

It's daylight now and as I don't have to go out anywhere I'm feeling a little calmer. I feel in the right frame of mind to tell you everything in detail.

No one knows exactly what happened. But what the police did tell us was that they crashed into a lorry which was coming towards them. They'd obviously been trying to overtake a car and hadn't seen the lorry coming.

Knowing what those two were like and judging by the mood they were in when they left (Loli by the way agrees with my theory) the two must have been larking around and flirting with the passengers of passing cars. They must have been driving alongside other vehicles, waving at their drivers and wolf-whistling. Of course, this would have distracted them from seeing the oncoming lorry and...

That's how they were killed as was the lorry driver who'd been transporting oranges to the border. The three of them were incinerated in the flames. It was impossible to identify them: with only a pile of cinders to work on there were of course no distinguishing traces. Reduced as they were to ashes, the only recognisable objects around them were a string of oranges scattered on the road like a splintered rosary of dashed hopes. The forensic scientist asked for the scant ashes to be divided into three parts and that one should be given to each family concerned. I myself couldn't think of anything more romantic. Separated though they were, I'm sure all three are to be blissfully reunited in one shared resting place.

As I think about it and mourn your exile, too, tears course down my cheeks like ephemeral pearls. How sad that these shall never console me by solidifying into a necklace, a remembrance of both you and them...

I'm still crying like Mary Magdalene herself. But endings, these days, are never happy. How I wish it might end like Darling Lily. Do you remember?

Life is not what it used to be!

The hearse carried two wreaths. One of them, a beautiful arrangement of red flowers, was from Masona and bore the message, "GOODBYE QUEENS". When we saw it attached to the back we all broke down in tears, fools that we are. The other wreath was from us. Made of yellow and red carnations, it was inspired by our flag. Its sash read, "TO TWO GLORIOUS RAINBOWS".

Behind the priest and his attendants was a procession of black-hatted, black-veiled friends and relatives. A background of rain and grey skies perfectly matched our mood.

I've just remembered what Lita always used to say to me when she felt depressed or down at heel: "Sure as hell we'll get to Heaven by car!" Lita's mother, as lanky as Lita (God rest her soul) had eyes full of tears and wore a short black mantilla and a dark-coloured dress. Clutching her arm was Washingtona's mother, fat like Washingtona herself. She wore a black veil which covered her face and touched the ground and which barely muffled her profuse sobbing. It would have been quite impossible to silence so much sorrow, so much grief. As I accompanied them, we were all so dejected and haggard with grief anyone would have thought that rather than going to someone else's funeral we were leaving our own.

As soon as Loli-Cock arrived at the cemetery, she and Lita's mother hugged each other, so fond are they of one another. Loli lost her mother when she was very young and so she could understand the extent of her friend's pain and distraction. I can't describe just how tearful the scene was. They were like two estranged sisters finally reunited after years of solitude and alienation.

La Masona, with characteristically ostentatious melancholy, sliced the air with enigmatic gestures, spraying it histrionically with the purple grain of grasses she had plucked from gravestones and which she kept in a tiny pomander. That done, she disappeared discreetly, silently.

Seeing the wet earth fill their graves and heaps of flowers covering the mounds, feeling too the rain against my face, I was suddenly overcome. This was my last contact, if you could call it that, with my friends. I couldn't stand it any longer: I left their mourning mothers and friends praying, a sprawling, black spider of a congregation; left them to the sepulchral church, its reverberating echoes of exasperation and grief, its wails of torment, its heady smell of candles.

Why is it, Aurelio, that we queens only have our mothers? I'll keep you briefed on anything else that happens.

Write to me.
Love, Lulú

(Written on the back of a post card from Palais Chaillot, Paris)

Aurelio,

Greetings from Amparo Iturbi. I'm in Paris doing some piano recitals. Tomorrow I'm off to New York and then on to the West Coast. Shall I bring you an all-American boy? You can buy just about anything in the US, so I'm sure they're giving them away.

Love, Amparo
Paris, 5th May, 1976

LETTER 40
To Aurelio Santonja from Carlos Besada
Valencia, 16th May 1976

Aurelio,

I'm losing my head: I haven't seen Angel for weeks. I *must* see
him again. I've been searching for him, looking around all the
streets and alleyways of the area where I first saw him looking at
me alluringly. But I haven't seen him. I tried following my
instincts, looking for traces, my heart occasionally stopping
whenever I thought I'd seen him at a street corner or the door of
a bar. Criminals always return to the scene of crime, or so I
thought. But he didn't.

It's been an exhausting search. I could feel my legs giving way,
my hopes abating, my adventurous spirit realising that my
search had virtually gone on as long as I had known him. I felt he
was now just a ghost, a projection, a trail of mist rising from the
port where seagulls ride the waves and where the sight of
glittering fish is belied by the scum of the water washing the
harbour's edge. No, there was no trace of him and as I searched
so did my spirits sink, tangibly, daily.

What a fleeting image I have of him. A mere memory. Most of
all my sadness always brings me back to the thought of dying
alone. So much for hope. Past and future are now confounded
like the passage of seaspray which would have us believe in time
but which ultimately is absorbed and annihilated by the solidity
and impassivity of the sand.

Aurelio, I ask of you to break this spell, rescue me from my
obsession, restore my faith – at the moment I feel as if I'd die
unseen, like an actor leaving the stage on tiptoes.

He left me without explanations, without so much as a goodbye.
The musical score is over and never again will there be another
concert.

Carlos Besada

Dear Aurelio,

Did you know that Sit-on-my-Arse has come back from America crazier than ever? Every perversion under the sun has turned her into a monster. She's put Frankenstein quite in the shade. I think living in the States is enough to turn anyone into the kookiest eccentric. Suffice it to say he no longer fancies the kind of men that he used to. Instead he spends his time rooting around flea-markets for all manner of cylindrical and fetishistic objects, chair legs, medical instruments, plastic pipes to meet his needs – if you get my drift. From the little I managed to get out of him about his trip to the States, that exalted paradise of hi-tech, I learned that he met someone who made plastic and rubber sex-aids, the kind that act as a substitute or supplement to human sex. From then on, the crazy queen hasn't looked back.

Apparently the man in question – man? Beast? I'm not sure which is the better description – frequently fist-fucked him right to the elbow. She couldn't get enough of it. "You've got no idea how much I enjoyed it... I took it right up to his elbow!" (But the truth is that she was taken to hospital, probably half-dead, and after months spent recovering from fever and delirium, was sent home.)

Since then, in spite of her hospitalisation, her fetishism has gone from bad to worse. We're talking a love affair with garden hoes, rakes, curved candelabra, lampstands, door handles, wine and scent bottles, onyx lighters, a weird variety of fruits (used for

169

their peculiar irregularities) etc. Her attachment to these has got out of control and I doubt if any psychiatrist could now reason with her.

His eyes are so dilated now as a result of his excesses – as if his astonishment at his own feats had one day frozen into a permanent fixture – that they have altogether enhanced his looks. But as for all her new admirers she's lost interest. She only cares for isolated parts, feet, muscular arms, etc. These she caresses with such intensity and disproportionate passion that the people here, unfamiliar with such esoteric pleasures, run a mile. Last Thursday I saw her in the street and, quite matter-of-factly, she told me about someone or other's foot. The way she went on about it you'd have thought she was talking about someone she was in love with. What she told me was so extraordinary that I thought I was imagining it all.

"Such a sexy foot! Who could resist falling in love with it? But it's strange, it never *looks* at me. Of course, I keep winking at it, saying romantic things to it... but do I get any feedback? All I can say is that it's a very conceited foot... it must be so beautiful I can't understand what it sees in me!"

P.S. I've just come back from Juan's. When I got there the door was wide open and I could hear a deafening noise inside. The hoover had been left on in the middle of the bedroom floor and Juan was lying flat on his face, unconscious.

What a sight! The hoover's pipe was right up his arse and was sucking up his insides.

I rushed to switch it off. His bedspread was covered in blood and blood was spurting out of where the pipe joined the main part of the hoover.

Juan was only just breathing.

Very carefully, I began to pull the pipe out his arse... what I could of it anyway. As you can imagine I was shitting bricks. The *smell* in the bedroom and the *sight* of Juan's bloody face. I can't take my mind off it. Why, Juan, why did you do it? And then, Aurelio, I remind myself not to ask stupid questions...

Loli-Cock

LETTER 42
To Aurelio Santonja from Rosita the Pathetic
Valencia, 20th May, 1976

Aurelio, listen to me. Lulú is a *bitch*! It's about time someone told you what sort of person you're involved with. Only someone like her could have acted so disgustingly. She's taken my man, simple as that. Who does that whore think she is! How dare she think she can go around the world like a self-styled Doña Juan, taking whatever slice of the cake she fancies and breaking other people's hearts in the process!

My blood boils just to think of it. Of course, my Carlos is a gullible lad, a little angel, susceptible to and easily hypnotised by any old vile sorceress who should decide to ensnare him. He's so naive that he doesn't realise that no sooner is he used, than he'll be tossed aside like a fag-end.

The worst of all this is that it only took him four days to come home to mummy, contrite as Mary Magdalene, pleading forgiveness and asking him to bale him out. You know I don't like slagging people off but your darling Lulú wouldn't give her money away at gunpoint. She expects to get everything for free! It boils down to this. If you want a boyfriend, you bloody well have to pay for him! All we need is one of *those* to support!

Between you and me, I don't know what things are like abroad – but here, when it comes to financing a love affair, the sky's the limit! Every day the prices go up. It's monstrous! And I'm not talking about simple maintenance or basic expenses either. Give an inch and they take a mile – the biggest mistake is to give way to an initial demand for a pay rise. And then they go on strike to blackmail you. In short, if they can get away with it, they'd rather make the minimum effort for the maximum dosh. It's absolutely scandalous!

But Aurelio, we're so used to our boys, what would we do without them? Oh, I quite forgot to mention that what we give them is on top of their social security, their three-yearly increments and the money we give them on the 18th July. National Boyfriend day! That's where it all goes – State benefits or no State benefits! Oh aren't we such stoic and long-suffering mugs, all for the sake of getting our rocks off! And now the pressure's on with all these democratic and liberal airs and graces we've come to adopt – I mean this fashionable cause of wanting to free ourselves from our condition as an exploited sexual minority.

The more I think about it, the more I think us queens were better off under Franco. You'll be thinking what a cliché: "We were better off under Franco" Indeed! But in those days a pick up was a pick up and no messing around. You only had to go to Mar Street's supermarket and go up to the first guy you fancied and say:

"What do you say to a quick fuck?" (no strings attached).

When you'd had him, you knew there were plenty more. A veritable crop of students, too horny to feel inhibited, would come up with the goods (dirty talk and a yearning arse) and leave you feeling totally satisfied. And with a clear conscience that you had done your bit towards the formative character-building of some future Minister of State.

To get back to Lulú (I can't seem to get her out of my head), you've no idea how much I hate her. I'm sure the only reason why she took him away from me was to spite me. Of course, she had no intention of setting him up in a nice little flat by the German college – she's much too tight-fisted for that. She just did it to get my back up.

She'd been giving him the eye for days without my realising it, mentally undressing him, the callous bitch. To think that I, oblivious, was saying things like:

"Lulú, it's lovely to see you!"

"Lulú, darling, why don't you help Carlos choose me a pair of shoes – you've got such good taste!"

"Lulú, sweetheart, you wouldn't mind buying me some chocolate while you're at it..?"

And so insidiously, the bitch began to infiltrate what was until

172

then a blissful relationship, like an invisible canker, until it was no more.

How right my father was in saying that no town was safe without Fascists to protect it!

To think I'd been so happy, so unaware, so gullible. That's why I overlooked her calculated side. Lulú this, Lulú that, Lulú how wonderful. And then all of a sudden she does this to me. The tears, the horror of discovering I'd been duped, of finding how hideously gullible I'd been and worst of all that simultaneously I'd lost both lover and a friend.

You've no idea how upset I am. I've shut myself off from the world, a broken woman. Half-crazy, I spend the entire day sending out SOS letters and telegrams, glued to the radio hoping that I'll hear Doña Elena Sanchís' reply to my letter with the patience and perseverance that only a Christian like my mother could have taught me. Otherwise my only occupation is my needlework which I'm so absorbed in that I'm sure it'll cost me my eyesight.

Love from your depressed friend,
Rosita the Pathetic

To Aurelio Santonja from Violet Rascayú
Valencia, 6th June, 1976

Aurelio,

Like a group of old biddies we've gone for the day to the Vera
hermitage in the country set in the most fertile and lush scenery
with its dusty tracks from where you can still see in the distance
the vast elephantine, ever-expanding city left behind us. There's
a gentle breeze and the sun stings us with its deliciously hot rays.
The sheer greenery of the surrounding country has made us
converts to Nature!

After so much time spent living in the city on a diet of asphalt
and exhaust fumes, it's an eye-opening experience to see the
region we come from *au naturel*; indeed we think it our very own
queendom. Of course, you live so far from here now that you
probably don't remember it. The shooting of Carlos Besada's
film (about which I'll tell you more another time) was really an
excuse for us all to sit down to have a massive paella – authentic
wooden spoons and all – a carafe of wine, mineral water, a salad
(fresh vegetables, of course, as we picked the vegetables from a
garden here) and fruit as tender to the touch as your inimitably
smooth bum!

Carlos Besada was wearing a white summer suit, an Italian
Panama and the lushest oasis of a smile – a reflection in fact of the
purity of the country here which, as yet, is uncontaminated by
buildings, TV aerials and everything else that detracts from an
othewise wonderful *nostalgie de la boue*. Talking of nostalgia, I
really think the country makes us acknowledge our roots and
realise just how cheesed off we are with the city!

The darling little bridge, the fences round the alfalfa, the potato and tomato plants, the tomatoes climbing prolifically, riotously on their canes, the fan-shaped arrangement of palm trees, lofty, sublime as ancient ruins. It's all so pastoral, need I go on!

While Carlos attended to his make-up in preparation for the filming, we took advantage of the bounteous weather to undress, skip around the countryside like the happiest of goats, dive into the river, splash about, embrace, scatter the fields with jasmine and poppies, stripped from the fields, playfully nudge each other's arses with our cocks, give each other the most innocent blow jobs...

Meanwhile, two peasants, who'd been spying on us from a nearby swamp, suddenly rushed out enraged, chasing us and hurling stones at us as we fled. We ran like crazy as they screamed after us, "You fucking queers!" Defiant, we responded by laughing at them. Brazenly we flashed our cocks at them and generously pulled the cheeks of our arses back to give them a "sneak preview". "Come on," we shouted, "we know what you really want is a good screw!" Stones, meanwhile, whistled past our ears. Though we cackled we feared deep down that if they caught us *they'd* have the last laugh. We'd be lynched for defiling their Arcadian territory, executed publicly in the city centre for our wanton ways.

When we got back to the set, the filming had been interrupted because Carlos wasn't feeling well. The cameras were on hold and everyone fussed about Carlos's attack of the squitters. What a come down! Shitting, vomiting, Carlos, I ask you! He had to squat, you know, as there wasn't a toilet or anything remotely civilised like that in sight, save a hornet infested hole, screened only by a striped curtain. You should have seen him, his face ashen, his suit covered in shit stains. He was the picture of martyrdom, gaunt and emaciated as the most melodramatic El Greco Christ. The gorgeous pin-up we were so used to had suddenly been reduced to a dishevelled slob constantly doubling over, snapping in two almost, with the pain in his stomach.

We kept seeing him appearing white as a sheet and disappearing again as he rushed to have another shit. Flapping about in a mild panic, we attended to his every need. So strange to see our idol denigrated, humiliated in this way even if we knew that this was a freak occasion.

Aurelio, aren't we wicked! Mind you we wouldn't be ourselves, would we, if we couldn't have a good bitch about our friends!

Carlos was rushed to the nearest hospital, in a critical state of dehydration. To this day, none of us knows whether the fruit was to blame or the vegetables.

As we gathered all our bits and pieces together, who should arrive, accusing us of destroying their tomato plants but our two friends accompanied by the gamekeeper. While at play we'd been too carefree to realise that we'd basically laid waste to the surrounding plantations. We'd have been all night discussing whether or not it was our fault, if it hadn't been for a sudden torrential downpour which, quick as a flash, saw us on our way back home!

From the car, we looked back at the Elysian splendours of the countryside now far in the distance.

Carlos finally got over what was merely a spate of indigestion. I saw him this morning. At first the doctors thought it might have been typhoid but luckily it was nothing serious. The crew sends its regards,

Love from Violet Rascayú

LETTER 44
To Aurelio Santonja from Nina Foc
Valencia, 15th June, 1976

Aurelio,

I can tell you what happened as vividly as if it were happening now. It concerns my mother and my traitor of a boyfriend. One day I'll tell you all the details but at the moment, I've a mental block about it which stops me from doing so.

At the time my boyfriend was asleep.

There were voices to be heard mixed with the sound of footsteps approaching the main staircase that leads to the bedrooms. The heat was so oppressive that I was lying naked on my bedclothes with the window wide open.

Suddenly I heard a scream, a scream that still rings in my ears and pierces me like a bone digging into my throat.

I woke up and got up. Once out of bed, I went into the corridor through which you can get to the staircase and heard my mother's ferocious voice. As she spoke to him you could plainly hear her charasteristic sarcastic sneer only she can muster.

From the top of the staircase, I could see him from behind. He turned round. Yes, it was him, Aurelio. My heart beat like crazy, my hands went to my chest as I could feel it virtually bursting out of my body. "Look at him," I said to myself, "what a two-faced bastard!" How could he have sworn his love to me but pissed off the moment my back was turned. It was as if the world was caving in on me, like an awful Leluch film, in which my poor mother played a star role.

My senses were scrambled. I could feel my emotions split down the middle as if I'd been sliced in two.

I could see my mother turn her back on him as she walked over to a cocktail cabinet. Esteponato, you're going too far! How could he have dared to rifle through my mother's bag when she was right there?

He took out a fistful of 1,000 peseta notes.

It's as if my mother's fifty years had aged her as quickly as she poured her glass of whisky into her frosted Murano tumbler, scarcely steadied by the alcoholic tremor of hands.

My eyes misted over with tears which began to fall down the staircase as if amplified, as if suddenly snowballing into boulders which would crush the scenario below!

I could see the *ending* in sight. The classic Hollywood formula which, without us realising, we so often try to translate into real life and emulate. I mean the ending where tragedy is almost saved by a deus ex machina, I say almost because it arrives just too late on the scene.

At that point, I could hear the deafening sound of laughter as my mother turned to face him. I couldn't bear to watch the scene yet I couldn't tear myself away. When she actually *bit his lips*, I had to look away. Nevertheless, I heard her slapping him – my own cheek still stings to think of it and I can feel her ice-cold whisky, too, dripping down his face and mixing with the blood from just above his eyebrow where she'd wounded him with a sharp piece of glass.

Nerve-racked as I'd been before, no one could accuse me of being apprehensive now as I went down the staircase with my loaded pistol which I normally keep hidden in the furthest reaches of my writing desk. With immaculate accuracy, I took fire and destroyed that feeble man, that now fragile thing, which had once given my life a false sense of security.

Pity that Lana Turner will never know just how responsible she was for my actions that night – how years spent gazing ever since my childhood at the velvet of her lips and her stirring eyes has come to influence my behaviour, indeed corrupt it.

Worst of all, the knowledge that I shall never be her causes me untold pain. As I haven't been able to live like her I only ask that I be allowed to die in the twilight style of doom and serene magnificence which so accompanied Lady de Winter's death against a violet backdrop of passions, romances and fantasies

178

which, alas, are the irrevocable property of history.

Sometimes, Aurelio, the simple application of a beauty spot is always needed to enhance life. Who needs our humdrum, dreary psychodramas, our everyday traumas?

Write to me, Aurelio. Send me some news. You've no idea how much I miss you. Do you think you'll ever come back to Valencia? On second thoughts, that was a stupid question. I know only too well that would be impossible for you. I might go over to see you sometime, we'll see. But my mother is a constant worry to me, she's so restless it's driving me mad.

Well, Aurelio, make sure you write to me.
Lots of love,

Nina Foc

TELEGRAM
N 3567 Pal 28/34 Day.........Hour.........Pesetas
URGENT
LANA TURNER. STOP. MINK FLIES OVER SIDE EMPIRE STATE. STOP. INQUEST TO FOLLOW. STOP.

Vital communiqué Conchita Piquer

Aurelio, these terrorists are plaguing me, this is the second of these death threats. I'm terrified. What can I do?

LETTER 45
To Aurelio Santonja from Amparo Iturbi
New York/Valencia, 25th June, 1976

Aurelio,

There's really not much you can say on a post card but you
know that neither my friend, Lucrecia Borgia, nor myself like to
write letters.How old-fashioned it is! You must realise also that
now I'm famous for my concerts I'm hardly ever at home. If I'm
not on a Jumbo, I'm winging my way from some country on a
Boeing. Two weeks ago I was on Concorde on a flight to Paris
via New York – amazing isn't it? As for my tour in Boston I
could write a comprehensive guide book. And you've no idea
how Victorian the queens there are. On the West Coast though
things were certainly different. When at Little Rock, I couldn't
help but cry a tear or two (you know how sentimental I am!).
And you should have seen how drunk I got in one of those clubs
where the bar disappears into the horizon like a great, swirling
sausage lit by the neon lights above. What a memorial to our
sweet Loreley, to our spiritual sister, our receiver of umpteen
roses...
    Now finally I'm back at home. What a relief! I found your
letters in the mail-box and I've spread them all in front of me. So
at long last I'm replying to you!
    You're the only person I ever write to and I'll definitely visit
you when I'm in Holland. We'll talk like old times, have a drink,
catch up on all our news.
    Things are going well for me at the moment. The American
public was charming. There was only one minor hiccup. I was at
the airport, waiting for Gate 14 to announce our departure, when

181

who should I see but two breathless platinum blondes, sliding about and teetering on Orly's slippery, mirror-like floors as they rushed in my direction, laden with luggage of all shapes and sizes.

"Oh," I muttered to myself, "they're getting nearer". As they did so I had to stifle a scream for fear of giving myself away. Terrified, I got out my sunglasses, managed in time to wipe them with a white tissue stamped with Orly Airport in avocado and put them on, just as they were about to pass me. I was right, it was Acrata Lys and Anarchy Gadé. Luckily they passed by without recognising me. My God, what a relief! I could breathe again! But I was nevertheless prepared to convert myself into a Doric column or an amphora-bearing caryatid if the need arose... The loudspeakers were making their announcement. "Pesagers plis gate number fortin," I repeated in my pidgin English. Suddenly I found myself in No Man's Land, in the final departure lounge with its duty free shops full of those disorientated tourists that I so love to watch.

It was time to pass through the customs and as I did so I cast nervous, sidelong glances around me, hoping and praying that I wouldn't be spotted.

I saw Anarchy Gadé go up to the customs officer, a mink coat wrapping one arm, her passport clamped in her mouth. Immediately in tow was Acrata Lys, struggling with an alligator which she dragged behind her on a chain. The alligator kept digging its heels in and I heard Acrata saying:

"Don't be so naughty, Ally, co-operate will you! I'll miss my plane at this rate. You miserable bitch, you've made me ladder my tights now!" Acrata got into a stew, the customs officer flushed with impatience, while I was about to throw up at any moment with my state of nerves. Sweat oozed through every pore and I couldn't even swallow. I thought of staging a Tolstoyesque faint but I didn't want to botch and end up with a broken neck and, besides, since all attention was on those two, I didn't think it worth risking doing myself an injury. Aurelio, you should have seen how they stole the thunder. They weren't just *attracting* attention, they were *monopolising* it.

The funniest thing was that the they hadn't changed the

photographs in their passports: they were still men! So, of course, the customs officer wasn't going to let them through.

"Listen, frog features, this is who we are. Enough's enough. It's a free country isn't it?"

"Ally, darling, bite this French dickhead will you – he's not letting us through."

The customs officer got no further than articulating, "C'est pas possible!"

With that they collared the manager, a man with an aubergine for a nose, who sorted the situation out for them immediately.

"Vous êtes Valenciennes?" he asked them.

"Transexuals – courtesy of Casablanca," they replied.

I don't know how it happened but they were allowed through, alligator and all!

We all got on Concorde and I managed to hide behind the air hostess. My heart throbbed painfully and I had to ask them for some Holy Water which, of course, they didn't have. They hadn't heard of Lourdes and from then on I couldn't take the esteem with which Concorde is held seriously.

The air hostess fanned me with a copy of (yesterday's) paper: I was still recovering from the shock of discovering that they were only sitting behind me. Horrified, I felt the back of my hair (by now extremely dishevelled) brushed by a fox tail accessory reeking of napthalene.

I kept thinking to myself, "Please, please God, don't let them see me. Our Lady of the Helpless, don't let them recognise me."

That's all I needed – those two in New York while I was doing my recitals and playing for the crème de la crème of New York's jet-set, a society noted for its serious devotion to culture. They'll ruin it all for me, I thought. Suddenly I realised that they'd twigged. Acrata Lys, screaming like a convent girl who's just started her first period, was pointing at me. They were both pointing at me – always a sign, I think, of how badly someone's been brought up – and, in a loud voice, quoted from *Variety*:

"De grit Catalan pianist, Amparo Iturbi."

I fainted! Every now and then I'd come to and hear voices, murmurs behind my back.

"Yoohoo! We know who you are!"

"If he's playing at Carnegie Hall, we must go. I'm sure he'll need our support..."

We were booked in at the same hotel so I was subjected to their life story.

"We've come over to attend some seminars on *Transexualism And The Class Struggle*."

And Acrata Lys, who's as thick as two short planks, said giggling:

"I didn't know that becoming a trannie meant going back to school!"

"Yes, Acrata," said Anarchy dismissively, "we're going for some group therapy sessions on Transexualism And Social Integration."

This was sure to be a tight schedule, since they were off to breakfast at Tiffany's and to have lunch at Carol Channing's. I rang up Carol, a friend of mine who I keep in contact with by letter, and told her that she should deport them or, among other threats, that I'd phone Lucille Ball and tell her Carol's age. That did the job very nicely – and all those years of loyal letter-writing really had paid off.

My concerts were a great success. Artist, diplomats, ambassadors, everyone was there. The crème de la crème honoured me with the exception of an embarrassing Gina Lollobrigida who was barred entrance because they thought she was a drag queen !

Love,
Amparo Iturbi

LETTER 46
(An unsigned fragment)
Valencia, 17th July, 1976

Aurelio, my precious,

Lulú, Sensurround and I decided to spend this week paying our friends visits. We haven't been in contact with many of them for ages and such are the pressures of modern life that there seems precious time these days to do what is now considered rather quaint and old-fashioned. But I think that's such a shame don't you? Think of all that gossip, intrigue and who's-been-to-bed-with-who that we miss out on. We used to do it so often – go for a gossip crawl, move on from one person's house to another's...

So first of all we went to Amparo Iturbi. Since her tour of North and South America, she hasn't been out at all. So here was our opportunity to catch up on all her news of her various encounters with the urban folk of both hemispheres.

As you can imagine we had to have tea and cake at five o'clock if you please. She studied at a girl's boarding school in Essex and so is a stickler for punctuality and ceremony, Baroque queen that she is. Lulú, who as each day passes becomes more outspoken and prone to give people a hard time, shot from the hip:

"Come on don't be so prissy, will you, Amparo. Can we get to the brass tacks. Tell all: what are the Americans like? What do they do in bed? What are their latest experiments in kinky sex?"

We tried to nudge her, appeal to her discretion: Sensurround is easily shocked, remember?, susceptible to choking on her cake. The colour rose to her cheeks. Yes, a piece of cake was lodged in her throat and we patted her back as she coughed and spluttered. Brazen Lola Glamour, mischief maker as always, wouldn't stop laughing. Amparo Iturbi meanwhile tried, like Greig Garson, to keep her chin up, to maintain her composure and the level of her teacup at a stately height as she held it elegantly, her pinkie raised, delicately arched, her posture not unlike that of an American aristocrat 'partaking' of tea at Buckingham Palace.

So was our week launched with its orgiastic cornucopia of confessions and confidences – an occasion without precedent, I might add for our stay-at-home, back-of-beyond Valencia. Read on...

LETTER 46
To Aurelio Santonja from Anarchy Gadé
Valencia, 18th July, 1976

Aurelio,

How happy we are! Acratita and I have at last made our wishes come true! We are now women through and through! You can't imagine how much we've gone through to turn dreams into reality. Yes, we finally made it to Casablanca and the operating table.

You should see us now: our breasts bulge with their silicon implants – topless showgirls at last! – and we've a darling vagina each! We're so thrilled we keep poking our fingers into it and anticipating the pleasures of penetration!

What a relief to be rid of those horrible, pendulous appendages. I'd much rather have been operated on without an anaesthetic but, alas, we were told that was out of the question. Anyway, the deed is done and I can't stop admiring the results if only to prove that it all really happened.

What rejoicing to have at last attained womanhood. I can hardly contain myself. I keep looking at myself in the mirror, touching my nipples, my tits, my darling little hole.

And then there's the endless possibilities of what I can do with my hair. Endless perming permutations, different pony tails, corkscrew curls, Bardot-style tresses, fringes – it's all too much! There's no stopping me as I flirt with myself, play the seductress, the exhibitionist, the courtesan, the impatient virgin. What fun it is, too, to play with my fanny and feel its feminine, rounded contours. Hang on a minute, I've just got to answer the doorbell and I'll be back...

It's six o'clock in the morning. I just can't wait to tell you about last night's events. What a night! The person ringing at the door was my friend, Acrata. She was wearing a frock finished at the neckline with the frothiest lace. She grabbed me by the lapels of my housecoat and said to me matter-of-factly: "Anarchy, darling... get some clothes on at once...we're going out!"

"No, no, no," I said, hand on hip, "I can't go out like this – it'll be the death of me!"

The overpowering fumes of Acrata's *Eau Sauvage* forced me back a few steps. "That's right, surprise me like this. It's all very well for you. You're dressed up to the nines. But look at me... I see, you just want to embarrass me you bitch. That's what you are, a slut, a whore."

Meanwhile Acrata acted dumb, played ingenuous, sucking her finger with the feigned innocence which I recognised as Brigitte Bardot's.

"You know very well that I need at least two hours to get changed and even then I'd only be doing it to please you."

What a cheek, I thought! To start with, going out into the street required a total makeover. I had to shower, give myself a leisurely treat of aromatherapy, as recommended by my masseur, hide last night's love bites (OK, a small price to pay for last night's little earner of 2,000 pesetas, I know), depilate my legs with my Ladyshave, pinch my cheeks, apply a touch of make-up in case I should happen to score (pale foundation, Maria Callas eyeliner, fuchsia lipstick), then think about my hair. I'd have to coil it into earphones and wear my wide-brimmed, voluminous hat with its extravagant spray of red roses.

Acrata, meanwhile, wouldn't stop yelling (I'm sure in her past life she was a town-crier) and talking about nothing in particular, going off on tangents, her pine kernel of a mouth piping up with pea-brained chitter chatter.

"And I said to him, no way," her anecdote went.

"Why not?" I replied, generously humouring her as I half-listened.

"Well, that's what I said but in fact there was no turning back and you know what it's like... I mean you only have to see a boy of his calibre, I mean size, I'm talking *diameter* here, to succumb... I was dumbstruck, my jaw dropped... words escaped me."

"Words escaped you?" I interrupted with bitchy incredulity.

"Well, only for a while," she went on, oblivious, "I mean it wasn't long before I'd grabbed it and had my mouth round it. Mmmmm! It had popped out of his flies like a jack-in-the-box and there I was swallowing it whole. There was no way of controlling it. It just *filled* me. There was no room to manoeuvre. Like having your first gobstopper. I couldn't possibly have talked if I'd wanted to... quite delicious. My gums were swimming with juice. I haven't tasted anything as delicious since my last plate of souquet. His cock was a deep colour, a dark, Pompeii red with prominent veins and every time my tongue licked them I could feel their blood boil till they throbbed... Carlos just stared at me like a half-wit, while the other man kept trying to silence my moans..." (Meanwhile I listened, quite prepared to believe any old thing. I had other crises to attend to. One of my false eyelashes was lopsided and I was getting into quite a flap over the fact that it wouldn't get into position.) "Then I heard the most frightful din. Carlos was suddenly buried under an avalanche of pots, pans, paella dishes, plates, cups and half a dozen champagne glasses, a present from my daughter-in-law. "Carlos, Carlos," I shouted, "they'll try to kill you... He'd caught us in flagrante delicto, but too stunned to do anything about it, then he started retaliating."

"Acratita, darling," I interrupted, "will you help me pull my zip up!"

While she helped me, I said. "How come Carlos was picking a fight, I thought you said he wasn't jealous!"

Of course, Acrata got all nervous, temporarily dropped the subject, made out that she'd clean forgotten the outcome. And what an innocent air she affected. Innocent, my foot! She was as calculating and underhand as ever – rather like someone who'd have stolen the thunder from Mme Curie and discovered radium while she was taking her siesta.

I'd finally dealt with my wayward eyelash. My waist was so cinched it was killing me, my arse felt as if it would burst at the seams as we left the bedroom. Acrata walked behind me, talked incessantly, wittering, gassing, babbling unintelligibly – I've never heard so much gibberish.

While she wore a lace-fronted frock, I'd donned a simple

189

evening suit cut so tight it felt as if it would split at the seat. This I'd teamed with a pair of shoes in the palest, most delicate shade of lime.

"Apart from being jealous, Carlos is a liar. What's more he's such a bungler. In fact he's got so little going for him that I can't see what Loli, your friend, could have possibly seen in him. But she's taken him away from me all the same, the bitch."

On and on Acrata went. I was up to the eyeballs of hearing her verbal diarrhoea, her problems – it was unbelievable just how long she could keep it up for. Of course, she hadn't told me where we were going – a gala for the presentation of literary awards, to be attended by the most illustrious local intellectuals. The Centenary of the Pen was the name of the prize-giving ceremony. You should have seen how many were there, close on a thousand and I'm not counting the waiters and photographers either.

So many well known people, Aurelio. The whole of Valencia's élite had shown up. You've never seen so many frocks. I don't know where they'd all come from. Even the most efficient couture house would have been hard pushed to run off such quantities single-handedly.

As to how we fitted in? Wonderfully. We mingled like a dream. Confident as models on the catwalk, we smiled graciously to the left and to the right, clocking up our acquaintances as we went. Wherever you looked, there they were, the self-appointed gentility. Categories were as follows: important people and by that I mean people who fancied themselves as such; less important people desperately trying to disguise their inferiority; nonentities smiling in awe of those who shouted just in case anyone had doubted their influence. In short, they were all lefties who happily, conveniently overlooked the incongruity of an ideology compromised by Bucks Fizz and foie gras canapés.

We, meanwhile, had no such pretensions. Our simple aim was to secure ourselves a boyfriend who would launch us, open doors for us in this worldly but intellectual milieu, the very equivalent to them of the awe with which we view the world of haute couture.

Appropriately, of course, he would have to be left-wing. OK, our tastes are expensive but our origins are appealingly humble. This of course was perfectly feasible: Acrata and I might as well have passed as disinherited Russian aristocrats, newly lionised after a period of dreary exile; alternatively as Deborah Kerr in *King Solomon's Mines*.

Being the Leos that we both are, heads turned everywhere we went. Inevitable really when you think of the flattering proportions of our false lashes!

Before we knew it, Acratita found herself swept up into the air by a group of admiring bearded journalists who took her to a cha-cha-cha party. I, meanwhile, held court to a circle of poets and belletristes whose eyes were on stalks at the sight of my silicon phenomena. "If they want a better look, they'll get it," I thought to myself as I sat blissfully ensconced. And I meant it. "Call themselves respectable?" I said to myself and out they came. My success was enormous. The crowd was breathtaken, aghast and to my surprise actually envious of what they saw.

From then on it was touch and go. I knew that if I took things any further, censorship would ensue. The ceremony would be over.

However liberal they were in prinicple, there would be limits. Besides, I knew only too well that my performance wouldn't be rewarded with mink coats or pearls. The situation was clear: I had to leave but not without a little sleight of hand. I'd nicked 12,000 pesetas worth of crisp banknotes from an unattended wallet and, for sentimental reasons alone, acquired a souvenir of leather-bound books.

It's time for me to kip now or I'll be keeling over. The excitement has been too much and I haven't had a bite to eat.

Love and best wishes from your soulmate,
Anarchy Gadé

P.S. Acratita isn't home yet. Of course, it goes without saying that she hasn't thought of sending word of herself let alone of giving you her love... but that's Acrata for you! A.G.

LETTER 48
To Aurelio Santonja from Lulú Bon
Valencia, 2nd August, 1976

Aurelio,

I've always thought that an educated queen is worth her weight in gold. So thought Bolchévique, too. The other day she went to a bookshop which stocks left-wing literature and bought *Das Kapital* (Carlos March was the author, or someone like that). At night when she thought she was quite alone she'd burn the midnight oil reading and seeing if she might not learn something from it in the process.

As far as I know though Bolchévique's capital is none the better for it. In fact, since the night her latest boyfriend ran off with all her jewellery, she is positively the worse off. He stole her year's savings too (hardly a fortune I might say though she would never admit it) and a string of cultured, Manacor pearls. She also lost a pair of silver earrings which her mother had given her for her birthday, some priceless old sovereigns, engraved with the heads of kings and queens and heraldic crests, a gold medallion with a picture of the Virgin Mary crowned with the tiniest, most beautiful diamonds and all her bracelets and coral armlets.

All her earrings and various trinkets went too. Although these were not worth much money, they were of great sentimental value, being a collection of presents which over the years her various boyfriends had given her. As the swine had watched how she'd signed her cheques in the bank all her savings and her budget for the month went as well. Other possessions to go were her darling Pekinese, her pink velvet mules (I don't need to tell you why she needed those!) her stereo and all her records – by

Sara, la Pradera, Olga, Chavela, Rafael, la Mota, la Feliu, la Mina, la Vanoni, Miguel Bosé and, of course, Julio Iglesias. My God, the boy had a nerve!

Since all of us are in league and staunchy loyal to each other we rang each other up and arranged to meet. Hilda de Perelló, Sanguijuela del Palma, Maruja Coño de Hierro, Sensurround and myself all got together. We were so worked up! Our blood boiled with disgust, our make-up no longer showed – our faces were so red with anger. Not even the Amazon's piranhas could rival our fury!

We couldn't believe it! He'd stolen her jewellery. There's nothing more intimate, more precious than someone's jewellery. It's something no one would exchange for all Heaven's riches.

Once we'd met up, we planned what was the most effective thing to do. It was our duty to stick together as friends and rally each others' support. We appreciate, of course, that for us queens a boyfriend is as indispensable as the Red Cross – indeed an institution, no less – but a boyfriend who decides to rebel and has the gall to meddle with the most intimate and lifelong part of our lives asks for revenge. Hence our major referendum and our call for the most vindictive action.

Our cry was for pursuit and capture. "WANTED" was our unanimous verdict and in the midst of a crisis our solidarity gave way to mirth. Indeed our screams of revenge must have filled the entire street outside.

But I couldn't help thinking, "What is to happen to our Bolchévique?" She can't go to the police station – no one takes *us* seriously. That was the bleak reality. Those pigs would sooner have us locked up than treat our cases with the respect due to law-abiding citizens like ourselves. Once inside those brutes would abuse us, beat our arses raw, kick us and at night, no doubt frustrated at still being on duty, gag us and fuck us like animals without our consent. The pleasure would have been entirely theirs because we could be sure that in the morning we'd be unable to sit down. Of course, if they'd only have the consideration to use a bit of Vaseline, it wouldn't have to hurt so much.

I can just imagine. Bolchévique with piles. But would they care? Four officers all queuing up for a gang-bang, ramming her, filling her, heedless of the suffering caused her. Bolchi ripped apart shouting, yelling...The four of them putting her through the mill, finally having to take her to hospital. And then the ignominy of hearing the bastards say that they'd found her like that in the street, that she was a pervert who deserved as good as she'd got, how all queens ought to be shot or sent to a psychiatrist for a dose of aversion therapy.

To get back to what Bolchévique was *really* going through though, she wept and wept, going from bar to bar – a fanfare of doom and gloom issuing from her wan lips. Yes, Bolchi a drunkard! And it has to be said, sympathy apart, that she actually wallows in her present predicament. She likes to suffer and wail for all the world to hear: "I loved my boyfriend! I want him back!"

The only thing the bastard left behind was her copy of Carlos March's *Das Kapital*. Sensitive soul that she is, she can't bring herself to look at it or read it, saying that it only upsets her because it reminds her of him.

As far as I could see the book isn't worth a second look. What is it anyway, some kind of cheap photo-novel anthology? Still Bolchi weeps as if it really were the end of time.

Needless to say she's already found herself another lover. It didn't take long for her to recover, did it? As for her new lover, she never mentions him. No doubt, he'll make off with whatever Bolchi has left which at this rate will have been reduced to the replacements for her mules. Her new lover, to all accounts, is quite a smoothie – and it's well known that he's got a string of others on the go as well. What a mess! To think that he'll be stealing from her, too. Serves her right anyway!

She now says she doesn't want to be known as Bolchévique: Sugar Daddy would be more fitting. Sarcastically, of course, since she says their distribution of labour is most unequitable, nights being the time when he recharges her batteries... at a price!

Nothing else to report, I'm afraid. I hope you write soon. What are you up to? I haven't heard from you for ages.

As you can see this is most one-sided. Here I am writing to you and what do I get in return?

All my love,
Lulú

194

LETTER 49
To Aurelio Santonja from Lulú Bon
Valencia, 3rd August, 1976

Aurelio,

Thin-lipped Carlos Besada, Alexandra Lake, a hanger-on who has settled into our group very nicely thank you, Juke-Box, responsible for Carlos' film score and I are on our way north to San Sebastián where we'll be fêting Carlos' success or commiserating his undoing.

I've already told you about the film Carlos made a few months ago, set in an imaginary Valencia which we all hope will one day be real. All your closest buddies star in it, plus a few others who you don't know but I'm sure you'd like to meet. Well, anyway, he's taking it to the San Sebastián International Film Festival and we're going by train – in fact some rattling contraption which barely deserves that name judging by our confused insides. But I'm really looking forward to the party... once we get there!

If only you were here with us. I think us Valencianas are hot news to those in San Sebastián. But then again I might be wrong. We could be notorious. Just imagine. A provincial bunch like ourselves painting the town red with our scandalous and pornographic display of Mediterranean camp. Who could wish for more!

We've heard a lot about those girls up north. But they're not the only attraction: there'll be people from all over the world. As we're going on a safari-style reconnaissance we've all kitted ourselves out in the most chic, khaki, paramilitary garb. (You can be sure that Deborah Kerr would be beside herself with envy!) If we're a success, so much the better. If not, it'll be their loss. But

I'm optimistic: for those northern girls a gaggle of Mediterranean exotics like ourselves are quite irresistible. No doubt about it, they'll be queuing up for more!

Didn't the barbarians come over at some point in history to despoil our lands. Well, there is some justice, because we'll be returning the visit, not to sack cities, of course, but to rape men!

The film Carlos is showing is something else. It's actually very simple: two upper-crust Valencian boys act as prostitutes by night, picking up men on Mar Street so that they can fund buying the aerosol cans with which they spray their regionalist liberation graffiti. One night they go around spraying graffiti in protest against the despotism of Castilian, the State's centralised policy of a single language for all. "DEMOCRACY FOR ALL", "LANGUAGE IS FREEDOM", "VALENCIAN FOREVER – CRACK THE MONOPOLY" were their pro-Valencian war cries, signed on behalf of Conchita Piquer, their regionalist heroine.

Well, just then the police appear on the scene and manage to catch one of them (played by Carlos). So as not to give away his friend and lover (a part played by Alexandra Lake) he denies all knowledge of the other boy – just like Jean Harlow in *China Sea*. Suddenly, as in a Griffiths film, revolution erupts all over the town. Rebels seize the town hall and besiege Government House, although the latter just manages to hold out. The police guarding Carlos are momentarily distracted and he escapes their clutches, arriving at the gates of Government House just in time to see it being successfully stormed. He runs inside but dies on the staircase from a mortal attack of syphilis. His friend finds him and cradles his lover in his arms.

History is made: Government House has fallen under control of the rebels and a great hush pervades the corridors and staircases of what was once the ancient seat of the Catalan monarchy. Their standard bearer covers Carlos' body with his flag, while Primitiva Livia pompously breaks into song with a rendition of the regional anthem. Placido Domingo overwhelms the assembled company with emotion, joining in with "New glories do we offer unto Spain..." Inspiring others, they all begin to sing in unison, roused by the stirring sentiments of "Comrades join arms one and all..."

Four men bear aloft the corpulent frame and tear-stained face of Carlos. "In workshop and fields alike, ring out..." they sing as they walk down Cavallers Street on their way to Mare de Deu Square. Along Miquelet Street to Reina Square, Corretgeria and Tapineria Streets and Rodona Square they intone, "Songs of love, psalms of peace..." And finally on their way from Llotja Arch to Mercat Square by the town hall – once known as Avenue Generalissimo Franco but now renamed after revolutionary hero Ansias March – the words, "Our triumphal march will honour our victory." At that, Carlos' body is laid down reverently on a magnificent mound, a form of funeral pyre, the Valencian flag fluttering above him. Thus does the film reach its emotional climax and the crowds, men and women sitting on each other's shoulders, by now exhausted from so much singing, declaim poems in honour of those who died that day. A procession of little boys in their First Communion sailor-boy outfits, missals and rosaries in their hands, gather round the corpse, scattering lilies and anemones in their wake. Millions of carnivalesque figures, black crêpe hanging from their high ornamental combs, mantillas draped round their shoulders in combination with the fluorescent donkey jackets of railway engineers, submerge the prostrate body of Carlos, a martyr to repression and a figurehead of hope, with their tears and flowers.

Dressed up to the nines in appropriately folkloric garb, Lo Rat-Penat, Miquelet, the new inhabitants of the town hall and activists and trade union members alike break into dozens of the most popular political anthems, among them *To The Barricades*, *International Amnesty*, *Till Death, My Lover*, and *Unfurl, Ye Flag!* Together we raise our arms proudly, fists and arms pointing skywards, heroes and heroines, triumphant queens celebrating the freedom to indulge a rainbow palette of anarchic make-up, to cross-dress, to cottage or rather come out of the water-closet and into society proper.

Suddenly, however, the shouting ceases. The crowds are awe-struck, incredulous, terrified. From high above, Our Lady of the Helpless, enthroned and surrounded by a cortege of cherubs and cloudlets, makes her gracious descent from the heavens, her aura at once limpid, ethereal, flamboyant, incandescent, solar, dazzling, divine, bewitching, even melancholy – her passage propelled by a celestial fanfare, the beating of drums, a dramatic retinue of thunder, lightning, hailstones, snowstorms, showers

197

and iridescent rainbows. The sky bountifully yields the falling mannah of countless confetti and peppermint pellets. Our Lady enfolds the corpse in her sumptuous mantle of embroidered damask, encrusted with its jewels and gems and gently carries it away to her heavenly dominion, far from all visible, earthly clouds, removed from sea, earth, sky, indeed from Heaven itself. Thanks be to God! The crowds stand by in silence, a silence so complete that a mere shudder would have broken it. In the softest, pearlised neon, the words THE END superimpose themselves on the scene.

As you can see, I think the film has all it takes to be a box-office hit. I'm sure it'll take the festival by storm. If not, no matter. We've plenty to do here – meet boys, screw around, bed the Basque male population and OD on sex. The world is our oyster, as I'm sure you'll agree.

The whole crew except for that wally, Alexandra Lake, send you their love – especially myself,

Lulú

LETTER 50
To Aurelio Santonja from Lulú Bon
Valencia, 8th August, 1976

Aurelio,

Everyone agrees that Nanci Night is one big headache: she's a gossip, an airhead, a shit-stirrer and what's more she loves to put the knife in. No amount of genteel Tunisian embroidery or crocheting – her favourite hobbies – can dissimulate her seamier side. Yes, once her needlework is done she unwinds by cruising the streets nightly – as her name befits – and scours the relevant parts of town in search of men, if necessary doing so until dawn. It has to be said she does it with a certain style: Nanci's hallmark is her fan which she flicks open and snaps shut with unrivalled aplomb.

Her latest find though has had gruesome consequences. She has actually got into her head that she wants to get *married*! No, I'm not making this up! She wants to make a sacrament of her love.

It has to be said Nanci is getting on. The advancing years are kind to no one and she herself isn't getting any younger.

She always tells people she's just turned thirty, but in fact she must be thirty-eight or nine. At this ripe old age people do start to think about settling down and of establishing somewhat resignedly, of course, a ménage of sorts.

The short term adventures of the past lose their appeal and give way to plans for the future in the form of finding a permanent, stable relationship, the security of an arrangement till death do us part. The main goal is to find oneself a reliable and faithful lover, a kind of armchair, if you like, to lie in during those long,

199

lonely winter evenings. Although I'm surprised that she's actually committing herself to the idea, I could see this coming. Fickle, fly-by-night that she is, she is now suddenly betraying all our beliefs and taking the cowardly option of a life of security and fidelity. How spineless her reaction at what is basically her disappointment in the gay scene – the reactionary collaborator!

Of course, when I heard about all this I wet myself laughing. But I soon calmed down and thought nothing of it. It just seemed unlikely that she'd really follow it up.

The story anyway is as follows. Nanci was walking down some street and a car – the kind of 50s style type you see in American films; remember Gina's Cadillac in *Anna Of Brooklyn*? – drew up beside her. A virile, seductive voice called out: "Hi there handsome, doing anything tonight?"

Nanci's attention was caught. "What a voice!" she thought, "so macho... and they're such a rare species these days, I'll never get the chance again!"

She turned round and, with feigned indifference, said: "What do you want, dear?"

Leaning over to the door of his car, opening it slightly to get her attention, Nanci's suitor invited her in.

"Sure!" she said.

Nanci examined him and thought: "My God, what eyes... and for a fifty year old, he's in fine fettle." And with that she stepped kamikaze-style into the passenger seat.

"Where shall I take you?" he asked.

Nanci Night was enthralled. She was in her element and, flicking open her fan, mimicked Marlene Dietrich's louche *Blue Angel*. Imperiously, resolutely, she ordered: "To the bullfight!"

Since then Nanci has been seen on many an occasion, walking with her future husband. The supercilious airs she has adopted have alienated and antagonised all her old friends who sneer and openly snipe at her in the street.

It really is common knowledge now that she wants to get married. Whenever we see her on the street she plays the grande dame. She's so stuck up and acts so constipated that it's easy to forget what's at the root of her behaviour. What happened obviously was that she must have woken up one day in a panic, thinking, "I must find myself a husband once and for all. If my mother could do it, I certainly don't see why I can't too..."

It got to the point where we had to dissuade her by force. We tied her to a chair until the poor creature slumped like a rag doll overcome with grief at finding her delusions of grandeur thus challenged. The disgrace was too much. To give up her man would be tantamount to suicide.

Poor Nanci cried and cried, imploring us.

"I don't want to stay single! I don't want to die single!"
Oh dear, the pain of solitude!
The pain of old age!
The pain of life itself!

Love and best wishes,
Lulú

INVITATION
PACO AND NANCI
WE'RE GETTING MARRIED!!!
WE ARE DELIGHTED TO INFORM YOU OF OUR
WEDDING AND REQUEST THE PLEASURE OF YOUR
COMPANY. THE CEREMONY WILL TAKE PLACE AT
PATERNA, 30th AUGUST, 1976

(Handwritten)

Our wedding list is at CORTY and LLADRO department stores.
We would so love you to come although it sounds very much like
you won't be able to make it.
Best wishes from Paco who looks forward to meeting you.
Lots of love from your friend, Nanci

(Post card from San Sebastián. Concha Boulevard)

Darling,

Carlos' film has been an extraordinary success! Carlos is beside
himself and is running up and down Concha Bvd, kissing
everyone he passes. Ecstatic, Alexandra Lake jumped off Mount
Iguelda – to an Icarus-like death. Juke-Box, pissed as a newt,
spends all day with a gang of Basque militia, singing that song
which goes something like, "Maite, I shall never forget you..."
While I've fallen in love with a member of ETA, who goes around
armed to the teeth *and* a guard posted outside Maria Christina
Palace. In short I'm having the time of my life!

Love from everyone,
Lulú, Carlos and Juke-Box

LETTER 51
To Aurelio Santonja from Lulú Bon
Valencia, 20th August, 1976

Aurelio,

The other day I was in my dentist's waiting room, and flicking through a copy of *Hello!*, when I read that Lana Turner's plastic surgeon said he couldn't give her another face lift because she'd run out of skin to pull back! The cruelty of ageing!

Talking of ageing, I'm reminded of the preparations for Nanci's wedding – or should I say *nuptials*! As a good friend of hers I've tried to pass on advice. But she won't hear of it. OK, it's her loss.

You should see the energy she's putting into sewing her trousseau (courtesy of her dowry), and the sheets for their wedding night. By the way, she doesn't want a purely practical bed, like the kind modern couples have, she's far too classical for that so she's given the sheets scallops. The pillows are of an open-work design so lovingly executed and so carefully matched to the style of the bed itself that the poor girl must have quite exhausted herself. One really must credit her for her ingenuity and good taste!

As for her nightdress, it is the most angelic creation of subtle tones and pastel shades, collar and cuffs finished with the most delicate white lace. The rest of her evening ensemble is calculated to be at the same time titillating and aesthetically sensational. Her knickers are of the sexiest organdie, her bra a mouthwatering shade of melon. Finished in crêpe de chine and embroidered with clusters of sequins, her garters, of guipure, in black and vermilion were imported especially from abroad. (Nanci and her beau went to Paris plundering the city for Dior – a sore point in fact as we're all so jealous.)

Her apartment is hung with Aubisson tapestries, her feet clad in slippers of chiffon, her boudoir full of sable hairbrushes. Trays of Sèvres porcelain are pretty dispensers for Nanci's many powder puffs. Otherwise accessories include platinum tweezers, fans of shantung silk and black lace which frame hand-painted images of Spanish majas and well-hung bullfighters, veils, ostrich feathers, pink peignoirs scented with heliotrope, ribbons, decorative flasks, an array of cosmetics and manicure sets, suspenders, silk stockings and, in the bathroom, towels and bathrobes, cherubs, dolphins and a round bath in black mosaic with taps in the shape of fishes in yellow gold. Nanci has had installed a bidet tailor-made to the shape of her seat and a lavatory whose bowl is concealed with a valance. When activated, music plays thus satisfying the demands of decorum and on all walls mirrors give the illusion of greater space. A shower which resembles an inverted Bernini fountain – a description which does no justice to its excesses – emits water in all directions and incorporates a light show which flashes on and off, converting Nanci's bathroom into a psychedelic disco!

Her cupboards of the most time-honoured oak burst at their joints with Vichy napkins, and tableware of every available design. These, woven of every conceivable material, include for rustic effect the red and white gingham of French bistrots. And, of course, as Nanci will tell you, no collection is complete without its Majorcan tablecloth, a cloth so labour-intensive to make that not even the nuns of Buen Remedio would be prepared to undertake the task.

Contents apart, you'll want to know more about the house Nanci's fiancé bought her. If I get carried away with detail you'll have to put my obsessiveness down to envy. Rather than a mansion, I'd say it was a palace. Situated on the outskirts of Valencia, in the residential area of Santa Barbara which is now so fashionable, it boasts a kidney-shaped swimming pool and a simple but elegant garden. Nanci's taste is, of course, very different to Loli's – the worst excesses of Puig are not for her.

Everyone knows how elegant and ladylike Nanci was, at one stage she might have trawled the streets but make no mistake her education was classy. She didn't go to Loreto school much as she'd have liked to, but to Pureza which, for a young child, is quite a feat.

I've dealt with the house but how about the master bedroom? If you haven't got an adequate picture of the place so far then a description of the bedroom's decor will do the trick. Furnished with a patrician splendour, its huge Queen Isabel wardrobe is of antique oak. A many-drawered bureau of burnished bronze, shining with fiery points of light, houses drawers, some open, some closed, all brimming with sumptuous clothes.

I only caught glimpses, Aurelio, but I could have died of envy. There were petticoats, silk slips, bras, lacy undies, tights and stockings in every imaginable shade. The bedroom ceiling is decorated with a mural depicting the horoscope, the bed a high-canopied four-poster with corkscrew poles supporting a tester festooned with the heaviest curtains of royal blue velvet.

But, Aurelio, this is only the half of it. Her decorating flair knows no bounds! What coquetry, what inspiration behind her collection of scent bottles, phials, flasks, exquisite ceramic and porcelain trays containing, as I mentioned before, every type of compact, powder puff and variety of cotton wool under the sun and, last but not least, a gigantic mirror framed in mother-of-pearl.

You should see Nanci now, in the flesh, as she combs her hair mechanically at her dressing table. The bride is nervous. She bites her lips and strokes her thighs with a sensuality now jaded by habit and over-indulgence.

Being the nosey creature that I am I couldn't help opening one of her fitted wardrobes. An avalanche of multi-coloured clothes threatened to spill out and I was forced to close it for fear of a sartorial landslide. It's early in the morning and the telephone's ringing. I can tell she's nervous: it must be her fiancé. I venture a sidelong glance, watch her finish off her shower and get dressed in a tick before she answers the phone. Dressed to kill in a fabulously expensive Rodier suit she bids me farewell, rushes downstairs and gets into her convertible.

206

The steering wheel is decorated with beads and tassels. The car revs up, she releases the handbrake and off she goes. She'll be at Puente Real by now, if her manic driving is anything to go by.

Lots of love,
Lulú

P.S. What's the big idea? Aren't you going to write to me or what?

LETTER 52
To Aurelio Santonja from Lulú Bon
Valencia, 28th August, 1976

Aurelio,

When a girl like myself relives, through writing these letters, the
follies of youth, I feel how time passes. This terrifying fact of life
leaves me with a bitter aftertaste.

At the end of the day it makes me realise how neither you nor
I are the same people who separated about a year ago. How time
passes! And how painful this separation! To experience its
legacy day in day out is like suffering perpetual castration! Pain
that trespasses on my peace of mind!

The past creeps up on me from behind, as if wrinkles were
first forming on my back and then spreading across the rest of
my body. But enough of these morbid thoughts! I should be
able to overcome these insecurities with pride and a positive
attitude.

From the carpet of my luxuriously furnished apartment, I pick
up a tiny speck of dust, a piece of confetti, perhaps from a bygone
party. I blow at it as if it were a rose petal which, fallen to the
ground, forecasts the coming bleakness of the winter months –
and resume my writing.

How little I know myself! How little I know you? Can we
really have lost contact with our past selves? I feel now like a
heroine of my time, fighting to the bitter end against the onslaught
of my adult years which weigh on me like a burden. Its biological
ravages seem not a thing of nature but an irksome artifice which
I can't get used to.

What now of hours spent making up, dressing up, in other

words, of cosmetic strategies designed to lure men to my bed?

Nothing is left save laddered tights in tatters and a heart whose emotions have gone to seed.

It took so long for the bra (a sartorial Peter Pan, if there ever was one!) to come to my notice that now, decrepit, tits sagging, I have only memories of times and adventures when youth seemed a permanent commodity. How those early years were kind! How they established a false sense of eternal youth!

Every day was like a Sunday, every day spent oblivious of time passing. Every night I usually think of you in my dreams but last night I dreamt I was Greta Garbo and that I was dying of an untreated breast cancer. It was a nightmare in which I knew I could longer hide from reality. I knew that you would never come back to me, come to my window, late at night, your silhouette joining the shadow of the door frame which falls across my bedroom window.

It makes me age just to think about it. Day after day your absence suffocates me. Whenever I want to play the piano, play the song you once composed for me, I just can't. My concentration flags, my willpower fails me.

I can tell from your recent letters that you no longer feel close to me. They have a certain detachment, a certain tone of indifference, as if they were written out of a sense of duty. Nostalgia, love, sentimentality are now no more than material for scientific recollection.

And I find it so hard to accept that your being away could conspire so against me.

I'd always thought that the crisis which made you decide to leave Valencia would ultimately bring us back together. And that, although the situation would never fully work itself out, you would fight against your initial decision and come back to me, for, in spirit, I will never leave your side.

I remember you as the only person capable of making something of this absurd life, of turning it upside down and shaking it, ridding it of its cobwebs. Without you Valencia is not the same!

You always fought against those who equated love, feelings, life with a bank balance of vested interests.

It is precisely this which needs redressing, this feeling that we are ciphers on a balance sheet.

After Eugenio's demise your letter-writing has slowed down. The ones you do write are sadder: they lack the calm and contentment of somebody who has done well to leave the homeland.

You haven't written one solitary line enquiring about your closest friend, Eugenio – unlike before when you always used to ask me to pass on messages. And how that made me jealous. You two were always so intellectual, so knowledgeable compared to me, an uneducated queen who'd grown up in the slums, with not a qualification to my name.

This change has affected me. I've repeatedly asked you if anything was the matter. But you won't come out with it. I reckon something must have happened but you won't tell me what it is.

On re-reading what I've written so far, I realise I've never written to you quite like this before, quite so seriously I mean. I've opened up, showed my vulnerable side, referred even to events which have virtually lost their significance now that I haven't heard from you for so long. But what is going through *your* head?

No one has heard any news from you. What do I care about those others, admittedly, save for the fact that if you haven't replied to their letters either, that means you're no longer interested in us. Otherwise, all I can think is that something dreadful must have happened.

For me a dreadful thing has already happened: your departure. The scene at the railway station might easily have precipitated a heart attack. To think how my temperament is dominated by the romanticism of tragic films, books, melodramas, all that romantic baggage nowadays considered silly and old-fashioned.

Have you ever found yourself gesticulating, jabbering to yourself incoherently, your heart seized up, your hands trembling, your eyes on the brink of tears, on the verge of taking your make-up with it as they course down your cheeks – well, that's exactly how I felt.

I feel quite old now after the many goodbyes we've said, goodbyes said on a railway platform which to this day reminds me of what I lost.

It makes me think there is nothing worse than prolonged goodbyes. And the less words exchanged the better. A wave will do, a wave, which as I recall, I saw off the train, as it left the platform, as it disappeared telescopically into the distance...

And as you disappeared, I was left standing with an overwhelming sense of grief – a bitterness which permeated my entire body in my sense of isolation.

How will we ever forget that bar on the station platform? There we were sitting opposite each other, unable to speak. Our worlds seemed to be falling apart. I felt as if I was going to throw up. On the table was my glass of coke, untouched, undrinkable. A fast exit would have been better; a pragmatic goodbye. I should have eschewed sentimentality. What good did it do to linger when the only certain future was to have a lover in exile?

I remember I touched your face with a trembling hand. What would I have done to have kept it there forever? As it was it was almost impossible to withdraw it. Your expression didn't help either. It was full of fear and apprehension.

One last kiss – and suddenly a vacuum!

As the train left at its more or less constant speed, my heart beat at a different, erratic rate. I was so depressed, so *frightened*.

As I thought of you you could read my feelings and I could tell your willpower was weakening as a result. What were you thinking that day? Did you suddenly regret leaving me in my unstable state? Were you suddenly overcome with ambivalence at the intensity of my feelings, at my state of helplessness?

What strange things emotions! Tears, torment, happiness, even the neutrality of the heart's biological pace seem to come from the same source – yet all are contradictory. On that day your emotions, too, must have been pulled in as many directions.

I remember how later on, when I tried to call you, and when the operator said your number was unobtainable, I fainted in the phone box. All I can remember, before blacking out, was a feeling of being cut by the cleanest, most impersonal knife wound.

I've spent many a night on the platform fantasising about your return. I'd get a shiver at the nape of my neck imagining that you were standing behind me. But in reality I saw only the rear end of a train, then a car momentarily enveloped by its exhaust fumes, the sight of a fatuous neon sign or the irritating blankness of the night sky.

Having said all this, Aurelio, I do feel a bit better now.

Our love will at least be saved from the dry rot which destroys so many other relationships. No, there's no chance of mutual boredom setting in! Meanwhile, we must remain faithful to each other, keep the ardour of our love as alive as it once was. Our air-mail letters will keep the coals burning, I'm sure. So keep writing, write to me soon, don't neglect me – that more than anything would be the death of me.

Whenever I think of you, Phaedra's Greek song comes to mind:

> *"To you I offered milk and honey;*
> *You, in return, poison gave.*
> *Yet as with an eagle striking airs aloof,*
> *Such pride as yours I recognise as but a veil."*

Lulú

To Aurelio Santonja from Lulú Bon
Valencia, 30th August, 1976

Nanci, nicknamed Night, is to be married today. What a fuss, you
might say, all for a wedding! More to the point, what a waste of
time. The house is packed with guests. As you can imagine,
discretion is the party's theme! Everyone is quite unashamedly
nosing about cupboards and drawers. Nanci, meanwhile, loves
the attention of her adoring, albeit competitive clique. As her
conservatism outweighs even that of Doña Germana de Foix's,
she has asked of her husband that he respect all Valencian
customs appropriate to the occasion. He, ever deferential, has
generously given her, quite apart from what I've already told
you, her bed, her mattress, her bolsters, her bedspreads and an
entire gold-plated bedroom suite. No luxury bridal item has
been spared.

And as Nanci wants to wear the traditional wedding-dress of
a Valencian wife-to-be, her wish has been granted. The dress is
fitted with skirts of the richest silk brocade; their white ground
is embroidered with flowers; her petticoat, which protrudes as a
deliberate design feature, is of black satin; a shawl knotted
stylishly about the waist is neat enough to pass as a cummerbund;
an apron of finest muslin is not only bordered in gold but also
scattered with shimmering sequins. Her fiancé has also given her
white silk stockings and a pair of slingbacks fronted with the
most elegant bows. Woven into her hair are bands of cloth which
pull back (the better to show off her cheekbones)! These in turn
are held in place by pins and slides, the whole arrangement
providing a decorative base for a high, ornamental, Valencian
comb (inspiration 15th century Vatican) in which are etched and

213

tooled in relief a picture of a house round which a sinister bat mysteriously flutters. Valencian superstition maintains that the symbol, an incongruously pagan one if I may say so, offers protection to whosoever wears it. From her earrings hang three rows of tiny pearls and adorning her neck a necklace of the most exquisite pearls accompanies a gold pendant on which pearls and emeralds vie for attention. A neckerchief in antique lace completes the picture. Oh, and I forgot to mention her shoulder-length black veil which she's supposed to wear as she makes her entrance into church. But if superstition is to play any part in this I doubt she will be able to wear so pious an accessory. The very act is bound to provoke the wrath of God, in whose name the tradition is held. And of course, such hypocrisy would incite the entire village to turf her out of the church, whereupon she would be duly stoned in the village square.

But to get back to the ceremony. It was an intimate affair, held in the bridegroom's private chapel in Paterna. Afterwards a formal reception was given, attended by all of Nanci's friends.

In the evening, they took off for Palma de Mallorca for their honeymoon, no doubt leaving behind them a trail of tin cans and pink loo paper on the motorway.

As for you, Aurelio, why haven't you written? Silence is far from golden – delay not.

Lulú Bon

TELEGRAM
N 1446 Pal 24/22 Day 30 Time Pesetas
COULDN'T GET IN TOUCH EARLIER. STOP. AURELIO
SANTONJA GARCIA DIED LAST WEDNESDAY. STOP.
THOUGHT TO BE SUICIDE. STOP. OVERDOSE OF
BARBITURATES. STOP. FAMILY WHEREABOUTS
UNKNOWN. STOP. FUNERAL IN HANDS OF SPANISH
EMBASSY. STOP. MY COMMISERATIONS. STOP.
SIGNED
ROGER SALVAT

LETTER 54
To Aurelio Santonja from Lulú Bon
Valencia, 2nd September, 1976

Aurelio,

What's up? Why haven't you written? Has the damp from
Amsterdam's canals so afflicted you with rheumatism that you
can't pick up a pen? Here the summer heat is so suffocating that
we've had to get the hell out of the city and, as the village fiestas
have begun, we thought we'd go round visiting all our friends
who live in the villages where it's all happening. Our Mini is
packed with the latest in summer fashions – any excuse to
épater the simple village folk. We've already visited Mary Sky
Stiu in Catarroja where they were involved in that macho fiesta
where men gather in a cul-de-sac and fire rockets at each other,
the test being to see if they can stand still without flinching. The
whole thing was utter madness: we ended up running away as
fast as our legs could carry us, crazy rockets chasing us as we
fled.

The funny thing is that these men are all queens underneath.
As far as macho posing is concerned they lay it on thick, but when
it comes to the evenings they become as camp as you or I. The
lesson I've learnt from all this is not to be taken in by all this
studied strutting. They're no different to the rest of us.

Our journey took us on to Alicante where we've been stopping
off at every village where flags and bunting announce some
fiesta or other.

One Saturday night we went to Sueca to visit some friends –
in fact Sueca is full of them – and to Cullera's discos. Cullera has
been fighting for autonomy and it looks as though they've

succeeded. Mary Sky Stiu, who's been with us since Catarroja and surprised one and all with how horny she is, took us over to the village where her boyfriend lives.

The village is in fact a little hamlet near Gandía, where quite by chance I met the most stunning, gorgeous boy I'd ever seen. His name is Angel Doñat and he looks the type of country lad who wouldn't hurt a fly. He's very earnest and charming and beautiful with it. We successfully abducted him and he's joined us on our travels. I'm head over heels, Aurelio! There I was resigned to never having another boyfriend, when all of a sudden here I am engrossed in an affair. Attentive and meek as the boy Jesus, he administers to my every need: I catch him looking at me with a candour that betrays unswerving devotion. But why, I wonder? What's the appeal? Perhaps he thinks me glamorous because I come from the city. In the evenings he clings to my side and although the weather's very hot I let him do so because of the pleasure our intimacy gives me. This feeling of being in love has done me a power of good. I feel so happy suddenly as if I've had a new lease of life. Angel is strong and kind at the same time – and he's mine. As I listen to the things he whispers in my ears I feel as if I've recovered the love that until now I thought I had lost irrevocably on that fateful day you left for Amsterdam. You had always understood me so well and known that I was one of those types who likes to have the best of both worlds – go out with somebody *and* screw around. But at the moment, monogamy suits me just fine. In Angel I have everything I need.

I'm writing to you from a village in the Valldigna region; I have totally lost all sense of space and time. (God knows how I managed to date this letter!) I've lost track now of which villages we've been to, which fiestas we've taken part in and of the drinks we've drunk and the drugs we've taken. At the moment we're living as though there's no tomorrow. As I write Angel nibbles at my ear; in fact temptation is getting the better of me if you get my gist...

Aurelio, I'm in love!
Lulú Bon

LETTER 55
To Aurelio Santonja from Lulú Bon
Denia, 4th September, 1976

Aurelio,

Still no word from you. Yet here I am writing to you come what may! We're in another village now, to the south of Denia. At the moment I think of nothing else but Angel and how much I love him. I'm sure you'd be asking me about him yourself if you were still writing to me.

You'll think this a cliché but his eyes are green, his hair the gold of ripe corn and when he smiles, his teeth are like a string of pearls. All right, I'm being kitsch, but you know what it's like to be a girl in love... I drool only to look at him. I'm sure I'd die if he left me. I'm so confident of his love and of his fidelity that in the little time I've known him I've allowed myself to take him for granted. I quite happily ogle at other men in the village in the knowledge that he won't retaliate. Long-suffering Angel looks at me dolefully while I have to make a conscious effort to keep my feelings to myself and not go over to him and say:

"Cheer up, darling. You don't think I'd leave you, do you?"

But I manage to restrain myself and carry on playing the femme fatale as I have always done anyway. At night, as I hold him in my arms and feel his naked body next to mine, I think, perversely: "If he left me I'd lose my mind!" As the night progresses I cling more and more closely to him. Muscular though he is, I could snap him in two from so much squeezing.

In the darkness of our bedroom, his eyes look searchingly into mine – two luminous headlights, two lasers in a room otherwise pitch black.

I could never tire of stroking his lips, his arse, his legs which are as hard as steel. I love to stroke his downy hair which tickles my hands as I do so.

As I write to you now, Angel is looking at me with a disconcerting intensity. He looks vexed. Then he asks me as if he has had to pluck up the courage to do so: "Who do you write all these letters to at night?" Ever intent on being enigmatic, I don't reply. Then, his look still perturbed, he carries on staring until he finally rests his head on his pillow. But I know that he's only *pretending* to sleep, that in fact he's waiting for me to join him.

I, too, am waiting to hear from you and hope you write soon.

Love from an ever naughty Lulú

LETTER 56
To Aurelio Santonja from Lulú Bon
La Safor, 5th September, 1976

Aurelio,

Since we've been in Benidorm things haven't been too great between Angel and myself. Put it this way we're not on speaking terms. For the first time he actually lost his temper at my antics. I'd obviously gone too far with my flirting. He came up to me one day and said that if I didn't stop behaving like this he'd push off. To begin with I took no notice. I've never liked being told what to do but he became so adamant, making no bones either about protesting in front of my friends, that I told him he could go to hell. At that he burst into tears and, taking what I'd said literally, promptly left me. I must say I was quite shocked and at the time didn't know what to say to him.

The next day, I combed the streets of Benidorm in search of him. I still only half believed that he'd left me. Yet I was dizzy from shock and the possibility that this might be it. No one had seen him. Some said that they may have seen him on a bus, others said they weren't sure if they'd seen him at the station... My friends wanted to leave Benidorm and go south to Alcoi and Elx but I wouldn't hear of it. I could think only of what might have happened to Angel – at worst that he had perhaps done something silly. So I decided to stay behind another day and, thanks be to God, I received a phone call from Angel. He was at Tavernes Beach and told me that he would be waiting for me there at which I heard him burst into tears. I caught the first bus and I was there in a flash.

You just can't imagine what sort of a state he was in and how much he cried when he saw me. We hugged each other and it felt as if we had known each other for years. I suddenly came to appreciate the joy of reunion and relief at the end of our dreadful separation. Although the wound was now healed, it left me with a feeling of how inextricably linked are the contradictory feelings of love and pain.

Reunited thus we spent two days together in bed, without stirring from our room. During that time all we drank was champagne....

Today we went to a neighbouring village for its first day of fiestas. Some patron saint or other is the cause of celebration but there are so many of them I couldn't tell you who she is or which underdogs she is affiliated to. The village was surrounded by orange trees and, on the horizon, an impressive mountain range dominated the landscape.

Night began to fall and the village square buzzed with an orchestra which provided its audience with the rhythms of rumbas and the cha-cha-cha. Suddenly I saw some friends from Valencia appear out of nowhere. They were all dressed up and the villagers were looking at them like zoologists confronted by an unknown species. I couldn't help it, I had to attract their attention. Shouting, screaming, finally plucking a feather from one of their headdresses, I began to shower them with greetings. "Darlings, lovely to see you, etc etc..." I let fly a volley of exuberant compliments, obscenities, Valencian in-jokes by which time the villagers really didn't know what had hit them. We were talking nine to the dozen, catching up on all our news, when suddenly I realised Angel was nowhere to be seen. The boy was driving me berserk. All my friends had wanted to meet him, and none of us knew where he'd gone. Had I upset him *again*? I didn't see how I could have.

But after a bit I started to think I really must have upset him. So I asked around to find out if anyone had seen him but no one knew of his whereabouts. I started to search in the bars but they were so packed it was like trying to find a needle in a haystack. Finally I gathered from someone that he'd last been seen making his way to the orange groves, near the Bay of Garaffo.

The night was clear and starlit and there was a full moon. I

221

suddenly started to get quite worried and I could feel my heart beating uncontrollably fast.

I left the party and started off in the direction of where I thought Angel might be swimming. The moon lit the way and the gravel on the path lining the ditches alongside the orange groves shone phosphorescent, reflecting the moon's glare, like scattered crumbs.

The green of the orange trees had turned black by night but its uppermost leaves were perforated with a halo of orange light, radiating from the village square.

In the distance, the mountains would suddenly bleach, go a ghoulish green or sulphurous yellow depending on which fireworks happened to illuminate them with their many-coloured sparks and scintillations. In fact, Nature itself seemed to be celebrating, taking part in the fiesta, too: as the orchestra filled the air with its trumpet blasts and drum beats which, amplified, carried right across the valley, reverberating and echoing as they went, so did the mountains flash in unison.

And you should have heard the crickets chirring, virtually screaming, terrible as the scream of Janis Joplin dying.

As I walked alongside the olive groves I was oblivious to my lover's unheard calls. The cool air of Gafarro Bay filled the atmosphere, taking the edge off the stifling heat.

I could hear a group of croaking frogs suddenly held in check as I passed. I started calling out to Angel. But there was no answer. The bay stretched before me, smooth and glistening. I sat at the water's edge and, touching it with my hand, watched it run through my fingers. Voices from the villages could be heard even at this distance. The party had finished and the young men and women of the village had gone up to the groves to pinch melons. Then they went for a midnight swim and would surely stay to sleep on the beach until the cool morning breeze woke them up. I heard laughter and the sounds of kids at play. It was then that I saw floating towards me on the black water, his body, upside down, a vision of rigor mortis.

At first I just didn't react.

My hand had gone to my mouth as if to stifle a scream but scream came there none. I was paralysed, my gesture redundant.

I was filled with fear, and my body was suddenly emptied of feeling but for the most acute pain.

"Why won't you speak?" I implored. "Why are you playing at being dead?" My attempts at mind over matter had been mere fantasies. The words articulated themselves fully conscious of what had happened. HE WAS DEAD. So started my despair and its endless repercussions.

The crickets went silent and it was as if the night went into mourning. I'll never know how many seconds, minutes, hours passed before I finally reacted. Then when they arrived, when the villagers knew, I was holding him in my arms cradling him like an exasperated mother who clutches a stillborn child to her bosom.

The boy's body smelt of the night's damp, rheumy air. No matter how many kisses I gave him he refused to come to life. Death had nipped his early years in the bud. We were both suddenly estranged, abandoned in the appalling vacuum left by death. My brain was numb. My only thoughts were why had he done it, for whom? Then guilt began to rack me. What if I hadn't done this...what if I hadn't said that? I was besieged by self-questioning.

All round me people stared at me in a state of shock. I heard someone whisper in someone else's ear: "No, no! Sssh! can't you see he's not dead!" Yes, I thought, deluding myself for a minute, he's just unconscious.

Nobody dared utter the word I so hoped to hear: suicide.

It was very early in the morning when the police arrived and tried to tear Angel away from my arms. I resisted, crying invisible tears of blank despair. They insisted, trying to reason with me. But I just couldn't part with him. He was like a son to me, a lover, a husband, all wrapped in one.

The forensic scientist in Valencia said that he'd swam out too far and drowned but I don't believe it. They're all just trying to whitewash what happened for fear of scandal. I know perfectly well that it was suicide and that I am to blame for his decision.

To think I am my own murderer! I shall never be able to live again with a clear conscience. Aurelio, how I need you now. Why, why don't you write to me?

GMP books can be ordered from any bookshop in the UK, and from specialised bookshops overseas. If you prefer to order by mail, please send full retail price plus £1.50 for postage and packing to:

GMP Publishers Ltd (GB),
P O Box 247, London N17 9QR.
For payment by Access/Eurocard/Mastercard/American Express/Visa, please give numberand signature.
A comprehensive mail-order catalogue is also available.

In North America order from Alyson Publications Inc.,
40 Plympton St, Boston, MA 02118, USA.

In Australia order from Stilone Pty Ltd,
P O Box 155, Broadway, NSW 2007, Australia.

Name and Address in block letters please:

Name
_____

Address
_____

_____

_____